SANDERS

EDGAR WALLACE

PAN BOOKS LTD : LONDON

First published 1926 by Hodder & Stoughton, Ltd.
This edition published 1948 by Pan Books Ltd..
8 Headfort Place, London, S.W.1

TO THE MOTHER

OF PENELOPE

I

THE MAGIC OF FEAR

I

ALL this happened in the interim between excellencies, or it could hardly have happened at all.

His Excellency, the retiring Administrator of the Reserved Territories, had departed amidst the banging of guns and the playing of the national anthem by a small band of near-white musicians, all of whom, and especially the cornet, had a tendency to play flat. The new Excellency was enduring the agony of gout at his house in Budleigh Salterton in Devon, and his departure from home was indefinitely postponed.

A change of administration made little or no difference to the people of the big river, and Captain Hamilton of the King's Houssas, for one, was hardly conscious of the lacuna as he strode savagely towards the hut which housed his youthful second in command.

His annoyance was well warranted, for Lieutenant Tibbetts had committed the unpardonable crime of writing to the newspapers—a weakness of his. Hamilton was moist and furious, for the afternoon sun blistered the world, and as he crossed the yellow oven-floor called a parade-ground, the heat of it came through the soles of his boots and tortured him.

The barrack hutments which formed one side of the square danced and shimmered in the heat haze; he saw the fronds of the Isisi palms in a blur; even the weaver birds were silent: when it grows too hot for the weavers to talk, it is very hot indeed.

Kicking open the door of Lieutenant Tibbetts's hut, he stepped in and snorted his disgust. Mr. Tibbetts, whose other name was Bones, lay face upward on the top of his bed; and he was arrayed in a costume beyond forgiveness, for not Solomon in all his glory wore purple pyjamas with alternate green and ochre stripes.

Hamilton flung down upon the table the paper he had been carrying as Bones opened one eye.

"'Morning, sir," he said, slightly dazed. "Is it still raining?"

"'Morning!" snapped Hamilton. "It is within an hour of dinner, and I've something to say to you, Bones!"

Bones relapsed into slumber.

"Wake up, and hide your hideous feet!"

The eyelids of the sleeper fluttered; he murmured something about not seeing the point—he had at least seen the newspaper, and recognised the Gothic title-piece.

"The point is, Bones," said Hamilton awfully, "nobody knows better than you that it is an offence for *any* officer to write to the newspapers on *any* subject! This"—he smacked the folded newspaper on the table—"this is an outrage!"

"*Surrey Star and Middlesex Plain Dealer*, sir," murmured Bones, his eyes closed, a picture of patience, forbearance and resignation, "with which, sir, is incorporated the *Sunbury Herald and Molesey Times*, sir."

His long body was stretched luxuriously, his hands were clasped beneath his head, his large red feet overhung the end of the bed. He had the air and manner of one who was deeply wronged but forgave his enemies.

"It doesn't matter *what* paper you write to——"

"'To which you write,' dear old officer," murmured Bones. "Let us be jolly old grammarians, sir, an' superior; don't let us go around debasin' the language——"

"Get up, you insubordinate devil, and stand on your big feet!" hissed the Captain of Houssas; but Lieutenant Tibbetts did not so much as open his eyes.

"Is this a friendly discussion, or isn't it, dear old sir?" he pleaded. "Is it a friendly call or a council of war, dear old Ham?"

Hamilton gripped him by the silk collar of his pyjama coat and jerked him to his feet.

"Assault!" said Bones quietly. "Mad with envy, captain strikes risin' an' brilliant young officer. Court-martial finds jolly old captain guilty, and he takes poison!"

"A newspaper man you will never be," said Hamilton. (Here Bones bowed gravely.) "You can't spell, for one thing!"

"Neither could dear old Napoleon," said Bones firmly, "nor dinky old Washington—spellin' is a sign of a weak mind. You're a good speller, I admit it, dear old Demos-thenes——"

"The point is this—and I'm perfectly serious"—Hamilton pushed his junior on to the bed, and he collapsed obediently—"you really must not write political articles, suggesting that the Secretary of State should come and 'see with his own eyes' "—Hamilton sought for the offending paragraph and read it—" '. . . the work that is being carried out by young officers unknown (except by the indigenous natives, who adore them) and unhonoured . . .'—of all the rubbish!"

Bones shrugged his narrow shoulders: his silence was offensively respectful.

"You'll not write any more of these self-advertising letters, Bones—either to the *Star*, the *Comet*, the *Moon*, the *Sun*, or any other member of the solar system."

"Let us keep religion out of the discussion, dear old Ham," said Bones in a hushed voice.

It is doubtful whether Mr. Nickerson Haben had even heard of the existence of that organ of public conscience, the *Surrey Star and Middlesex Plain Dealer*. He was not the type of man who gave a thought to any newspaper that had a circulation of less than half a million.

And yet, the appearance of this literary effort of Bones coincided with a peculiar moment of crisis in his life, and the sequel almost excused the subsequent jubilation of the *Surrey Star* and went far to consolidate the editor's claim that "What the *Star* thinks to-day, the Government does to-morrow!"

For Nickerson Haben went almost at once to examine the Territories with his own eyes. He was in the middle thirties and had the globe at his feet. How this came to be the case, nobody troubled to consider.

A narrow-chested and pallid man with heavy raven hair, one lock of which hung over his forehead in moments of oratorical excess, he was deep-eyed, thin-lipped, hollow-faced, and had hands white and long. Nickerson was swept into the House of Commons in a whirlwind of oratory that blew down a phalanx of sober men and conservative citizens which stood between. Silver-tongued, or glib, according to your political preju-dices, he carried his powers of suasion and criticism into the chaste and unemotional atmosphere of Parliament. So that Ministers squirmed uneasily under the razor-edge of his gibes, and the Whips, foregathering in the lobby, grew pettish at the mention of his name. A party man, he never fell into the error of wounding the susceptibilities of his own leaders; if he criticised them at all, he merely repeated, in tones of finality, the half-confessions of fallacies they had already made.

When a Government fell, Mr. Haben, deserting a safe seat, fought West Monrouth County, turned out the sitting member and returned to Westminster in triumph.

The new Government made him an Under-Secretary, first of Agriculture, then of Foreign Affairs. He had married the widow of Cornelius Beit, an American lady, fifteen years his senior—a clever woman with a violent temper and a complete knowledge of men. Their home life, though it was lived at Carlton House Terrace, was not happy. She knew him rather too well; his own temper was none of the sweetest. He had all the arrogance of a self-made man who had completed the process just a little too young. She once told a near friend that Nickerson had a streak of commonness which she found it difficult to endure, and there was even talk of a divorce.

That was just before her operation for appendicitis. The best surgeon in England performed; her recovery was never in doubt. Nickerson, under the spell of her recovery, went down to the House and delivered the best speech of his life on the subject of Baluchistan.

Three days later she was dead—there had occurred one of those curious relapses which are so inexplicable to the layman, so dreaded by the medical profession.

Haben was like a man stunned. Those who hated him —many—wondered what he would do now, with the principal source of income departed. They had time for no further than a brief speculation, the matter being decided when the will was read, leaving him everything— except for a legacy to a maid.

This tragedy occurred between excellencies, an opportunity seized upon by a sympathetic chief. Nickerson Haben went out on the first African mail-boat, to combine business with recreation; to find flaws and forgetfulness.

Lieutenant Tibbetts, of the King's Houssas, was the newsman of headquarters. The lank legs of this thin, monocled lad had brought many tidings of joy and calamity, mostly exaggerated.

Now he came flying across the lemon sands of the beach, a mail-bag in his hand, his helmet at the back of his head, surprising truth in his mouth.

He took the five steps of the stoep in one stride, dashed into the big, cool dining-room where Hamilton sat at breakfast, and dropped the bag into his superior's lap at the precise moment when Captain Hamilton's coffee-cup was delicately poised.

"Bones! You long-legged beach-hound!" snarled Hamilton, fishing for his handkerchief to mop the hot Mocha from his white duck trousers.

"He's coming, Ham!" gasped Bones. "Saw my letter, dear old sir, packed his jolly old grip, took the first train! . . ."

Hamilton looked up sharply for symptoms of sunstroke.

"Who is coming, you left-handed oaf?" he asked, between wrath and curiosity.

"Haben, old sir. . . . Under-Secretary, dear old Ham!" Bones was a little incoherent. "Saw my letter in the jolly old *Star* . . . he's at Administration now! This means a C.B. for me, Ham, old boy; but I'm not goin' to take anything unless they give old Ham the same——"

Hamilton pointed sternly to a chair.

"Sit down and finish your hysteria. Who has been stuffing you with this yarn?"

It was the second officer of the *Bassam*, he who had brought ashore the mails. Haben was already at Administrative Headquarters, having travelled on the same ship. For the moment Hamilton forgot his coffee-stained ducks.

"This is darned awkward," he said, troubled. "With Sanders up-country . . . what is he like, this Haben man?"

Bones, for his own purpose, desired to give a flattering account of the visitor; he felt that a man who could respond so instantly to a newspaper invitation appearing over his name must have some good in him. He had asked the same question of the second officer, and the second officer, with all a seaman's bluntness, had answered in two words, one of which was Rabelaisian and the other unprintable. For Mr. Haben did not shine in the eyes of his social inferiors. Servants hated him; his private secretaries came and went monthly. A horsey member of the Upper House summed him up when he said that "Haben can't carry corn."

"Not so bad," said Bones mendaciously.

Early the next morning Sergeant Ahmet Mahmed brought a grey pigeon to Hamilton, and the captain of Houssas wrote a message on a cigarette paper:

> *Haben, Foreign Office tourist, en route. He is at A.H.Q. raising hell. Think you had better come back and deal with him.*

Hamilton had gone out in a surf-boat to interview the

captain, and the character of Mr. Nickerson Haben was no longer a mystery to him.

He fastened the paper to the red leg of the pigeon and flung it up into the hot air.

"'Ware hawks, little friend of soldiers," he said conventionally.

2

Linked very closely with the life and fate of Mr. Nickerson Haben, Under-Secretary of State (this he did not dream), was that of Agasaka, the Chimbiri woman. Mr. Haben was dressed by the best tailor in Savile Row; Agasaka wore no clothes at all except for the kilt of dried grass which hung from her beautiful waist.

A tall maiden, very slim of body and very grave of eyes, no lover for any man, having a great love for something more imponderable than man; terribly wise, too, in the ways of ghosts and devils; straight-backed, small-breasted, beloved of children, so strong in the arm and skilled in her strength that she could put a spear beyond the range of young men's throw—this was Agasaka, the Chimbiri woman, daughter of N'kema-n'kimi, the dead woodman.

She was elderly for a virgin, being seventeen; had been wooed by men in their every mood; had kindness for all, generosity for none.

She lived with her brother, M'suru, the hunting man; and his women hated her, for she never spoke a lie and was frank to her elderly brother on the matter of their numerous lovers. They would have beaten her, but that they knew the strength of her throwing arm. Where hands did not dare, tongues were more reckless, but none of their mud stuck. Few men were so poor in mind that they would admit others had succeeded where they had failed.

She had lived for many years with her father in the deep of the forest in the abiding place of M'shima-M'shamba, the fearfully boisterous devil who tears up trees with each hand, whilst his mouth drips molten fire; and other mighty ones dwelt near by. N'guro, the headless dog, and Chikalaka-m'bofunga, the eater of moons—indeed, all except the Fire Lizard, whose eyes talk death. And N'kema had taught her the mysteries of life and the beginning of life and the ground where life is sown. She knew men in their rawness and in their strength. N'kema taught her the way in which she might be more wonderful than any other woman; the magic handed down from mouth to mouth—the magic which was old when they laid the first deep stones of the Pyramids. . . .

Men were afraid of her; even Oboro, the witch-doctor, avoided her.

For this was her strangest magic: that she had the power to bring before the eyes of men and women that which they desired least to see.

Once, a small chief stalked her by the river path where the grass is chin-high, having certain plans with her. And at the right and lonely moment he slipped from cover, dropping his spears in the grass, and caught her by the arms so that, strong as she was, she could not move.

"Agasaka," he said, "I have a hut in this forest that has never heard a woman's voice——"

He got so far and then, over her silken shoulder, he saw three black leopards walking flank by flank along the narrow path. Their heads hung low, their golden eyes shone hungrily.

In an instant he released her and fled to his spears.

When he turned again, leopards and woman were gone.

Aliki, the huntsman of her village, neither feared nor cared, for he was familiar with magics of all kinds and often walked in the woods communing with devils. One night he saw a vision in the fire, a great red lizard that blinked its heavy eyelids. Aliki looked round his family circle in a cold-blooded search for a victim. Calichi, the fire lizard, is the most benevolent of devils and will accept a deputy for the man or woman to whom, with its red and blinking eyes, it has given its warning of death.

This Aliki saw his three wives and his father and an
uncle who had come many days' journey on a hunting
trip, and none of these, save the youngest wife, was well
enough favoured for the purpose. Calichi is a fastidious
devil; nothing short of the best and the most beautiful
will please him. Beyond the group sitting about the red
fire and eating from the big pot that stood in the embers,
were other groups. The village street of Chimbiri-Isisi
runs from the forest to the river, a broad avenue fringed
with huts; and before each hut burnt a fire, and about each
fire squatted the men and women of the house.

Dark had come; above the tall gum trees the sky was
encrusted with bright stars that winked and blinked as
Calichi, but more rapidly.

Aliki saw the stars, and rubbed his palms in the dust for
luck; and at that moment into his vision came the second
wife of his neighbour, a tall woman of eighteen, a nymph
carved in mahogany, straight and supple of back, naked
to the waistline of her grass skirt. And Aliki knew that he
had found a proper substitute and said her name under his
breath as he caught the lizard's eyes. Thereupon the beast
faded and died away, and Aliki knew that the fire-god
approved his choice.

Later that night, when Loka, the wife of M'suru the
huntsman, went down to the river to draw water for the
first wife's needs, Aliki intercepted her.

"There is nobody so beautiful as you, Loka," he said,
"for you have the legs of a lion and the throat of a young
deer."

He enumerated other physical perfections, and Loka
laughed and listened. She had quarrelled that day with the
first wife of her husband, and M'suru had beaten her. She
was terribly receptive to flattery and ripe for such adven-
ture as women enjoy.

"Have you no wives, Aliki?" she asked, pleased. "Now
I will give you Agasaka, the sister of my husband, who is
very beautiful and has never touched the shoulder of a
man." This she said in spite, for she hated Agasaka, and

it is a way of women to praise, to strangers, the qualities of the sisters they loathe.

"As to Agasaka—and wives"—he made a gesture of contempt—"there is no such wife as you, not even in the hut of the old king beyond the mountains, which are the end of the world," said Aliki, and Loka laughed again.

"Now I know that you are mad, as M'suru says. Also that you see strange sights which are not there to see," she said in her deep, gurgling voice. "And not M'suru alone, but all men, say that you have the sickness *mongo*."

It was true that Aliki was sick and had shooting pains in his head. He saw other things than lizards.

"M'suru is an old man and a fool," he said. "I have a ju-ju who gives me eyes to see wonders. Come with me into the forest, Loka, and I will tell you magic and give you love such as an old man cannot give."

She put down her gourd, hiding it in a patch of elephant grass near the river's edge, and walked behind him into the forest. There, eventually, he killed her. And he lit a fire and saw the lizard, who seemed satisfied. Aliki washed himself in the river and went back to his hut and to sleep.

When he awoke in the morning he was sorry he had killed Loka, for of all the women in the world she had been most beautiful in his eyes. The village was half empty, for Loka's gourd had been found and trackers had gone into the woods searching for her. Her they found; but nobody had seen her walking to death. Some people thought she had been taken by Ochori fishermen, others favoured a devil notorious for his amorous tricks. They brought the body back along the village street, and all the married women made skirts of green leaves and stamped the Death Dance, singing strangely.

Aliki, squatting before his fire, watched the procession with incurious eyes. He was sorry he had killed the Thing that was carried shoulder high, and, dropping his gaze to the dull fire, was even more sorry, for the hot lizard was leering up at him, his bulging eyelids winking at a great rate.

So he had taken the wrong sacrifice.

His eyes rose, rested on the slim figure of a woman, one hand gripping the door-post of her brother's hut. And there came to Aliki a tremendous conviction.

The lizard had vanished from the heart of the fire when he looked down.

No time was to be lost; he rose and went towards the virgin of Chimbiri.

"I see you, Agasaka," he said. "Now this is a terrible shame to come to your brother's house, for men say that this woman Loka had a lover who killed her."

She turned her big eyes slowly towards him. They were brown and filled with a marvellous luminosity that seemed to quiver as she looked.

"Loka died because she was a fool," she said, "but he who killed her was a bigger. Her pain is past; his to come. Soon Sandi *malaka* will come, the brown butcher bird, and he will pick the eyes of the man who did this thing."

Aliki hated her, but he was clever to nod his agreement.

"I am wise, Agasaka," he said. "I see wonders which no man sees. Now before Sandi comes with his soldiers, I will show you a magic that will bring this wicked man to the door of your brother's hut when the moon is so and the river is so."

Her grave eyes were on his; the sound of the singing women was a drone of sound at the far end of the village. A dog barked wheezily in the dark of the hut and all faces were turned towards the river where the body was being laid in a canoe before it was ferried to the little middle island where the dead lie in their shallow graves.

"Let us go," she said, and walked behind him through an uneven field of maize, gained the shelter of the wood behind the village, and by awkward paths reached the outliers of the forest, where there was no maize, for this place was too sad for the weaver birds and too near to the habitation of man for the little monkeys who have white beards. Still he walked on until they made a patch of yellow flowers growing in a clearing. Here the trees were very high, and ten men might have stood on one another's heads against the smooth boles, and the topmost alone could have touched the lowermost branch.

He stopped and turned. At that second came an uneasy stirring of the tree tops, a cold wind and the rumbling of thunder.

"Let us sit down," he said. "First I will talk to you of women who loved me, and of how I would not walk before them because of my great thoughts for you. Then we will be lovers——"

"There is no magic in that, Aliki," she said, and he saw that she was against him and lifted his spear.

"You die, as Loka died, because of the word which the lizard of fire brought to me," he said, and his shoulder hunched back for the throw.

"I *am* Loka!" said the girl, and he looked and his jaw dropped. For she was truly Loka, the woman he had killed. Loka with her sly eyes and long fingers. And she had Loka's way of putting a red flower behind her ear, and Loka's long, satiny legs.

"Oh, ko!" he said in distress, and dropped his spear.

Agasaka bent in the middle and picked it up, and in that moment became herself again. There was no flower and her fingers were shorter, and where the sly smile had been, was the gravity of death.

"This is my magic," she said. "Now walk before me, Aliki, killer of Loka, for I am not made for love, but for strange power."

Without a word the bemused man walked back the way he had come and Agasaka followed, and, following, felt the edge of the spear's broad blade. Though she touched lightly, there was a line of blood on her thumb where blade and skin had met. The wood was growing dark, the wind was alternately a shriek and a whimper of sound.

Near the pool at the edge of the forest she swung the spear backward over her left shoulder as a cavalry soldier would swing his sword, and he half turned at the sound of the whistle it made. . . .

The first wife of her brother was by the pool gathering manioc root from a place where it had been left to soak—the head of Aliki fell at her feet as the first flash of lightning lit the gloom of the world.

3

The sun was four hours old when a river gunboat, a white and glittering thing, came round the bluff which is called The Fish because of its shape. The black waters of the river were piled up around its bows, a glassy hillock of water, tinged red at its edges, for the *Zaire* was driving against a six-knot current. Every river from the Isisi to the Mokalibi was in spate, and there were sand shoals where deeps had been, and deeps in the places where the crocodiles had slept open-mouthed the last time Mr. Commissioner Sanders had come that way.

He stood by the steersman, a slim and dapper figure in spotless white, his pith helmet at a rakish angle, for an elephant fly had bitten him on the forehead the night before, and the lump it had induced was painful to the touch. Between his regular, white teeth was a long, black cheroot. He had breakfasted, and an orderly was clearing away the silver coffee-pot and the fruit-plates. Overhead the sky was a burning blue, but the glass was falling with alarming rapidity, and he desired the safe harbourage of a deep bank and the shelter of high trees which a little bay south of Chimbiri would give to him.

"Lo'ba, ko'lo ka! A fathom of water by the mercy of God!"

The sleepy-eyed boy sitting in the bow of the boat drew up his wet sounding-rod.

Sanders's hand shot out to the handle of the telegraph and pulled, and Yoka the engineer sent a clanging acknowledgment.

"Half a fathom."

Thump!

The boat slowed of itself, its wheel threshing astern, but the nose was in sand and a side-swinging current drove the stern round until it was broadside to the sand-reef. Then, as the wheel reversed, the *Zaire* began to move towards the right bank of the river, skirting the shoal until the nose found deep water again.

"Lord," said the steersman, virtuously annoyed, "this bank has come up from hell, for it has never been here since I was without clothing."

"Think only of the river, man," said Sanders, not inclined for gossip.

And now, above the tree-tops ahead, Sanders saw the rolling smoke of clouds—yellow clouds that tumbled and tossed and threw out tawny banners before the wind.

And the still surface of the river was ripped into little white shreds that leapt and scattered in spray. Sanders moved his cigar from one side of his mouth to the other, took it out, looked at it regretfully and threw it over the side. His servant was behind him with an oilskin invitingly held; he struggled into the coat, passed his helmet back and took in exchange the sou'wester, which he fastened under his chin. The heat was intolerable. The storm was driving a furnace blast of hot air to herald its fury. He was wet to the skin, his clothes sticking to him.

A ribbon of blinding light leapt across the sky, and split into a tracery of branches. The explosion of the thunder was deafening; it seemed as if a heavy weight was pressing down on his head; again the flash, and again and again. Now it showed bluely on either bank, vivid blue shrieks of light that ran jaggedly from sky to earth. The yellow clouds had become black; the darkness of night was on the world, a darkness intensified by the ghastly sideways light that came from a distant horizon where the clouds were broken.

"Port," said Sanders curtly; "now starboard again—now port!"

They had reached the shelter of the bank as the first rain fell. Sanders sent a dozen men overboard with the fore and aft hawser and made fast to the big gums that grew down to the river-side.

In a second the deck was running with water and the Commissioner's white shoes had turned first to dove-grey and then to slate. He sent for Yoka the engineer, who was also his headman.

"Put out another hawser and keep a full head of steam." He spoke in coast Arabic, which is a language allowing of nice distinctions.

"Lord, shall I sound the *oopa-oopa* *?" he asked. "For I see that these thieving Akasava people are afraid to come out into the rain to welcome your lordship."

Sanders shook his head.

"They will come in their time—the village is a mile away, and they would not hear your *oopa-oopa*!" he said, and went to his cabin to recover his breath. A ninety-knot wind had been blowing into his teeth for ten minutes, and ten minutes is a long time when you are trying to breathe.

The cabin had two long windows, one at each side. That to the left above the settee on which he dropped gave him a view of the forest path along which, sooner or later, a villager would come and inevitably carry a message to the chief.

The lightning was still incessant; the rain came down in such a volume that he might well think he had anchored beneath a small waterfall, but the light had changed, and ahead the black of clouds had become a grey opacity.

Sanders pulled open the doors he had closed behind him; the wind was gusty but weaker. He reached out for a cheroot and lit it, patient to wait. The river was running eight knots; he would need hand-towing to the beach of the village. He hoped they had stacked wood for him. The Chimbiri folk were lazy, and the last time he

---

* Siren. On the river most words describing novel things are onoma-topœic.

had tied they showed him a wood stack—green logs, and few of them.

Yoka and his crew loved to hear the devil whoop of the *oopa-oopa*—Sanders knew just how much steam a siren wasted.

His eyes sought the river-side path—and at the critical moment. For he saw eight men walking two and two, and they carried on their shoulders a trussed figure.

An electric chrysanthemum burst into blinding bloom as he leapt to the bank—its dazzling petals, twisting every way through the dark clouds, made light enough to see the burden very clearly, long before he reached the path to stand squarely in the way of eight sullen men and the riff-raff which had defied the storm to follow at a distance.

"O men," said Sanders softly—he showed his teeth when he talked that way—"who are you that you put the ghost mark on this woman's face?"

For the face of their passenger was daubed white with clay. None spoke: he saw their toes wriggling, all save those of one man, and him he addressed.

"M'suru, son of N'kema, what woman is this?"

M'suru cleared his throat.

"Lord, this woman is the daughter of my own mother; she killed Aliki, also she killed first my wife Loka."

"Who saw this?"

"Master, my first wife, who is a true woman to me since her lover was drowned, she saw the head of Aliki fall. Also she heard Agasaka say 'Go, man, where I sent Loka, as you know best, who saw me slay her.' "

Sanders was not impressed.

"Let loose this woman that she may stand in my eyes," he said, and they untied the girl and by his order wiped the joke of death from her face.

"Tell me," said Sanders.

She spoke very simply and her story was good. Yet——

"Bring me the woman who heard her say these evil things."

The wife was found in the tail of the procession and

came forward important—frightened—for the cold eyes of Sanders were unnerving. But she was voluble when she had discovered her voice.

The man in the streaming oilskins listened, his head bent. Agasaka, the slim woman, stood grave, unconscious of shame—the grass girdle had gone and she was as her mother had first seen her. Presently the first wife came to the end of her story.

"Sandi, this is the truth, and if I speak a lie may the 'long ones' take me to the bottom of the river and feed me to the snakes!"

Sanders, watching her, saw the brown skin go dull and grey; saw the mouth open in shocking fear.

What he did not see was the "long one"—the yellow crocodile that was creeping through the grass towards the perjurer, his little eyes gleaming, his wet mouth open to show the cruel white spikes of teeth.

Only the first wife of M'suru saw this, and fell screaming and writhing at her husband's feet, clasping his knees.

Sanders said nothing, but heard much that was in contradiction of the earlier story.

"Come with me, Agasaka, to my fine ship," he said, for he knew that trouble might follow if the girl stayed with her people. Wars have started for less cause.

He took her to the *Zaire*; she followed meekly at his heels, though meekness was not in her.

That night came a tired pigeon from headquarters, and Sanders, reading the message, was neither pleased nor sorry.

High officials, especially the armchair men, worried him a little, but those he had met were such charming and understanding gentlemen that he had lost some of his fear of them. What worried him more were the reports which reached him from reliable sources of Agasaka's strange powers. He had seen many queer things on the river; the wonder of the *lokali*, that hollowed tree-trunk by which messages might be relayed across a continent, was still something of a puzzle to him. Magic inexplicable, sometimes revolting, was an everyday phenomenon. Some of it was crude hypnotism, but there were higher things beyond his understanding. Many of these had come down through the ages from Egypt and beyond; Abraham had brought practices from the desert lands about Babylon which were religious rites amongst people who had no written language.

The *Zaire* was steaming for home the next day when he sent for Abiboo, his orderly.

"Bring me this woman of Chimbiri," he said, and they brought her from the little store-cabin where she was both guest and prisoner.

"They tell me this and that about you, Agasaka," he said, giving chapter and verse of his authority.

"Lord, it is true," said Agasaka when he had finished. "These things my father taught me, as his father taught him. For, lord, he was the son of M'kufusu, the son of Bonfongu-m'lini, the son of N'sambi. . . ."

She recited thirty generations before he stopped her—roughly four hundred years. Even Sanders was staggered, though he had once met an old man of the N'gombi who told him intimate details about a man who had lived in the days of Saladin.

"Show me your magic, woman," he said, and to his surprise she shook her head.

"Lord, this one magic only comes when I am afraid."

Sanders dropped his hand to his Browning and half drew it from its leather holster.

He was sitting under an awning spread over the bridge. The steersman was at the wheel, in the bow the *kano* boy with his long sounding rod. Purposely he did not look at the woman, fixing his eyes on the steersman's back.

His hand had scarcely closed on the brown grip when, almost at his feet, he saw the one thing in all the world that he loathed—an English puff-adder, mottled and swollen, its head thrown back to strike.

Twice his pistol banged—the steersman skipped to

cover with a yell and left the *Zaire* yawing in the strong current.

There was nothing—nothing but two little holes in the deck, so close together that they overlapped. Sanders sprang to the wheel and straightened the boat, and then, when the steersman had been called back and the sounding boy retrieved from the cover of the wood pile where he crouched and trembled, Sanders returned to his chair, waving away Abiboo, who had arrived, rifle in hand, to the rescue of his master.

"Woman," said Sanders quietly, "you may go back to your little house."

And Agasaka went without the evidence of triumph a lesser woman might have felt. He had not looked at her —there was no mesmerism here.

He stooped down and examined the bullet holes, too troubled to feel foolish.

That afternoon he sent for her again and gave her chocolate to eat, talking of her father. She was sitting on the deck at his feet, and once, when he thought he had gained her confidence, he dropped his hand lightly on her head as he had dropped his hand on so many young heads.

The puff-adder was there—within striking distance, his spade head thrown back, his coils rigid.

Sanders stared at the thing and did not move his hand, and then, through the shining body, he saw the deck planks, and the soft bitumen where plank joined plank, and then the viper vanished.

"You do not fear?" he asked quietly.

"Lord . . . a little; but now I do not fear, for I know that you would not hurt women."

The *Zaire*, with its strange passenger, came alongside the residency wharf two hours before sundown on the third day. Captain Hamilton was waiting, a fuming, angry man, for he had been the unwilling host of one who lacked something in manners.

4

"He's pure swine," said Hamilton. "Nothing is good enough for him; he raised hell when he found you weren't here to meet him. Bones mollified him a little. The silly ass had a guard of honour drawn up on the beach. I only found this out just before the boat landed, and it was too late to send the men to quarters. But apparently it was the right thing to do; Nickerson Esquire expected it—and more. Flags and things and a red carpet for his hooves and a band to play 'Here comes the bride!'"

All this between wharf and residency garden. A figure in white stretched languidly in a deep chair turned his head but did not trouble to rise. Still less was he inclined to exchange the cool of the broad veranda for the furnace of space open to a red-hot sun.

Sanders saw a white face that looked oddly dirty in contrast with the spotless purity of a duck jacket. Two deep, suspicious eyes, a long, untidy wisp of hair lying lankly on a high forehead—a pink, almost bloodless mouth.

"You're Sanders?"

Mr. Haben looked up at the trim figure.

"I am the Commissioner, sir," said Sanders.

"Why weren't you here to meet me; you knew that I was due?"

Sanders was more shocked than nettled by the tone. A coarse word in the mouth of a woman would have produced the same effect. Secretaries and Under-Secretaries of State were god-like people who employed a macrology of their own, wrapping their reproofs in the silver tissue of stilted diction which dulled the sting of their rebukes.

"Do you hear me, sir?"

The man on the chair sat up impatiently.

Hamilton, standing by, was near to kicking him off the stoep.

"I heard you. I was on a visit to the Chimbiri country. No notice of your arrival or your pending arrival was received."

Sanders spoke very carefully; he was staring down at the scowling Nickerson.

Mr. Haben had it on the tip of his tongue to give him the lie. There was, as the late Mrs. Haben had said, a streak of commonness in him; but there was a broader streak of discretion. The gun still hung at the Commissioner's hip; the grip was shiny with use.

"H'm!" said Mr. Under-Secretary Haben, and allowed himself to relax in his chair.

He was clever enough, Sanders found; knew the inside story of the Territories; was keen for information. He thought the country was not well run. The system was wrong, the taxes fell short of the highest possible index. In all ways his attitude was antagonistic. Commissioners were lazy people, intent on having a good time and "their shooting." Sanders, who had never shot a wild beast in his life, save for the pot or to rid himself of a pressing danger, said nothing.

"A thoroughly nasty fellow," said Hamilton.

But it was Bones who suffered the heaviest casualty to his *amour-propre*.

Left alone with the visitor in the hour before dinner, Bones cunningly led the conversation towards the *Surrey Star and Middlesex Plain Dealer*.

"I suppose, sir, when you read my jolly old letter, you thought I had a fearful nerve?"

"Your letter?" Mr. Haben allowed his head to fall in Bones's direction.

". . . about seeing the place with your own holy old eyes," and Bones went on, unconscious of the doom which awaited him, and explained fully his reason for writing, the thought that led him to write, the incident that induced the thought.

"My good young man, you don't imagine that His Majesty's Government would send a Minister of State flying off to Africa because an empty-headed subaltern wrote letters to an obscure county journal, do you?"

Bones opened and closed his eyes very quickly.

"I came—but why should I tell you?" asked Nickerson Haben wearily. "You may be assured that your letter had nothing to do with my coming. As I said before, you officers have too much time on your hands. It is a matter which requires looking into."

But it was at dinner that he touched the zenith of his boorishness. The dinner was bad; he hated palm-nut chop; sweet potatoes made him ill; the chicken was tough, the coffee vile. Happily he had brought his own cigars.

Bones spent that trying hour wondering what would happen to him if he leant across the table and batted an Under-Secretary with a cut-glass salt-cellar.

Only Sanders showed no sign of annoyance. Not a muscle of his face moved when Mr. Nickerson Haben made the most unforgivable of all suggestions. He did this out of sheer ignorance and because of that streak of commonness which was his very own.

"A native woman is a native woman," said Sanders quietly. "Happily, I have only had gentlemen under my control, and that complication has never arisen."

Mr. Haben smiled sceptically; he was sourest when he smiled.

"Very noble," he said dryly, "and yet one has heard of such things happening."

Hamilton was white with rage. Bones stared open-mouthed, like a boy who only dimly understood. The pale man asked a question and, to the amazement of the others, Sanders nodded.

"Yes, I brought a girl down from Chimbiri," he said; "she is at present in the Houssa lines with the wife of Sergeant Abiboo. I hardly know what to do with her."

"I suppose not," more dryly yet. "A prisoner, I suppose?"

"N-no"—Sanders hesitated—seemed confused in Haben's eyes. "She has a peculiar brand of magic which rather confounds me——"

Here Mr. Nickerson Haben laughed.

"That stuff!" he said contemptuously. "Let me see your magician."

Bones was sent to fetch her—he swore loudly all the way across the dark square.

"That is what we complain about," said Mr. Haben in the time of waiting. "You fellows are in the country so long that you get niggerised." (Sanders winced. "Nigger" is a word you do not use in Africa.) "You absorb their philosophies and superstitions. Magic—good God!"

He waggled his long head hopelessly.

"My poor wife believed in the same rubbish—she came from one of the Southern states—had a black mammy who did wonderful things with chicken bones!"

Sanders had not credited him with a wife. When he learnt that the poor lady had died he felt that worse things could happen to a woman.

"Appendicitis—an operation . . . fool of a doctor." Mr. Haben unbent so far as to scatter these personal items. "As I said before, you people—hum . . ."

Agasaka stood in the doorway, "missionary dressed" as they say. Her figure was concealed in a blue cotton "cloth" wrapped and pinned about her to the height of her breast.

"This is the lady, eh? Come here!" He beckoned her and she came to him. "Let us see her magic . . . speak to her!"

Sanders nodded.

"This man wishes to see your magic, Agasaka; he is a great chief amongst my people."

She did not answer.

"Not bad-looking," said Nickerson, and did a thing which amazed these men, for he rose and, putting his hand under her chin, raised her face to his. And there was something in his queer, hard eyes that she read, as we may read the printed word. The streak of commonness was abominably broad and raw-edged.

"You're not so bad for a nig . . ."

He dropped his hands suddenly; they saw his face

pucker hideously. He was looking at a woman, a hand-some woman with deep shadows under her eyes. It was the face he often saw and always tried to forget. A dead white face. She wore a silk nightdress, rather high to the throat . . .

And she spoke.

"Won't you wait until the nurse comes back, Nick? I don't think I ought to drink ice-water—the doctor says——"

"Damn the doctor!" said Nickerson Haben between his teeth, and the three men heard him, saw his hand go up holding an imaginary glass, saw his eyes fall to the level of an imaginary pillow.

"I'm sick of you—sick of you! Make a new will, eh? Like hell!"

He stared and stared, and then slowly turned his drawn face to Sanders.

"My wife"—he pointed to space and mumbled the words—"I—I killed her——"

And then he realised that he was Nickerson Haben, Under-Secretary of State, and these were three very un-important officials—and a black woman who was regarding him gravely. But this discovery of his was just the flash of a second too late.

"Go to your room, sir," said Sanders, and spent the greater part of the night composing a letter to the Foreign Secretary.

II

THE CLEAN SWEEPER

THE soldiers of the old king who lives beyond the mountains came down into the Ochori country and took back with them ten women and forty goats—and this was the year of the sickness, when goats were very valuable. And a week later they came again, and in yet another week they repeated the raid.

Mr. Commissioner Sanders sent an urgent message into the old king's country and journeyed to the Ochori to meet the old man's envoy. . . .

On a certain day, over the northern hills came Buliki, chief minister of the great king K'salugu-M'pobo, and he came with great *hauteur*, with four and sixty spearmen for his escort, and each spearman wore the leopard skin of the royal service—that is to say, a leopard skin with three monkey tails, signifying the swiftness, the ferocity and the agility of these men. He boasted that he was the fortieth of his house who had sat in the royal kraal and had given the law.

Sanders, with a more modest escort, waited in the city of the Ochori for the coming of this mission, which was two days late and was even now arriving, not at dawn as had been faithfully promised, but in the heat of the day. Sanders sat cross-legged on his canvas chair, chewing an unsmoked cigar and drawing little patterns with his ebony stick on the sand.

Behind him, tall and straight, his bare, brown back rippling with muscles with every movement, was Bosambo, chief and king of the Ochori folk north and south.

Behind the shelter which had been erected to serve as a palaver house was a section of Houssas, brownfaced men in blue tunics, handling their rifles with an easy familiarity which was very awe-inspiring to the dense mob of the Ochori people who had come to witness this memorable meeting.

Sanders said no word, realising that this was not the moment for confidences, and that in all probability Bosambo was quite as wise as he himself on the matter of the great king's delinquencies. For north of the hills was territory which was as yet independent, and acknowledged no government and no king beside its own.

Whether this was to remain so did not depend entirely upon the result of the interview, for no man knew better than Sanders that nothing short of four battalions could force the passes of the great mountains, and war was very unpopular with the British Government just about then.

The royal guard which the king had sent as escort to his minister wheeled on to the big square and formed a line facing Sanders, and the Houssas regarded them with the peculiar interest which soldiers have for possible casualties. Buliki was a big man, broad, tall and stout. He swaggered up to the palaver house without any evidence that he was impressed by the importance of the man he was to meet.

"I see you, white man," he said in the Bomongo tongue, which runs for six hundred miles to the north and the west of the Territories.

"I see you, black man," replied Sanders. "What message do you bring from your master?"

"Lord," said the man insolently, "my master has no message for you, only this: that whilst he rules his land he knows no other king than his own beautiful impulse and has no other law but the law he gives."

"Oh, ko!" said Sanders sardonically. "He must have a very powerful ju-ju to talk so boldly, and you, Buliki, have surely the stomach of a lion—for hereabouts I am the law, and men who speak to me in the tone of a master I hang out of hand."

His tone was bleak and cold, and his blue eyes strayed unconsciously to the high tree before the palaver place.

Buliki, who knew nothing of the sacred character of an embassy, went grey under his tawny skin and shuffled his feet.

"Lord," he pleaded, in a different voice, "I am a tired man, having come this day across the Mountain of the Cold White Powder that Melts. Therefore be gentle to me, a poor chief, who does not know the ways of white men."

"Go back to your master, Buliki, and speak this way: Sandi, who sits for his king on the great river, desires that no soldiers may come again from the king's territory to raid the women and goats of the Ochori. For I am a man quick to kill, and no respecter of kings or chiefs. I have ploughed little kings into the ground and the crops of my people have flourished on the bones of princes. Where is M'balagini, who brought his spears against me? He is dead and his house has rotted with the rains. Where is Kobolo, the N'gombi warrior who took his young men into battle against me? You will search the forest for his city, and his spirit weeps on the great mountain. Little kings are my meat: how mighty are they in the house of their wives! How small are they when I bring them in irons to my great ship! Go back to the old king and say this: The chief or soldier of his who comes this side of the Ghost Mountains shall be slaves for my people and be glad they are alive. The palaver is finished."

After the embassy had departed . . .

"Dam' nigger!" said Bosambo, who was blacker than a spade suit but had the advantage of a Christian education. "Silly ass! . . ."

Then, in his own language, for Sanders did not favour Coast English:

"Lord, this old king is very cunning, and there sits in the shadow of his hut a white man who knows the ways of white lords."

"The devil there is!" said Sanders in surprise, for this was news to him, that Joe had gone that way.

Up in the old king's country Buliki, prostrate and on

his face before the wizened old man, told the story of his embassy, and the king listened, stroking his thin, frizzly beard.

Joe the Trader (he had no other name) listened too, and had parts of the message translated to him.

"Tell the old man," he said to his interpreter, "that all that stuff is bunk! Say, Sanders ain't got no soldiers more'n fifty! Tell him that if he sends down to head-quarters an' complains 'bout these threats, Sanders'll get it in the neck—not allowed to do that sort of thing."

Joe, in his semi-sober moments, was an authority on what may be described as the unwritten laws of the wild. He had tramped up and down Africa from the Zambesi to the Lado, and he had learnt a lot. There wasn't a lock-up from Charter to Dakka that had not housed him. He had traded arms and gin for ivory in the days of Bula Matadi, and had drifted now to the one sanctuary where the right arm of any law could not reach him.

Of all the men in the world he hated best Mr. Sanders, and had good reason for his antipathy, for Sanders flogged the sellers of gin, and hanged even white gentlemen who purveyed Belgian firearms to the unsophisticated and bloodthirsty aborigines.

"Here! . . ." Joe was excited at the idea. "Tell him to send for Sanders to a great palaver—somewhere up the Ghosts—you'd get him coming up that road. . . ."

This plan was duly translated. The old king's dull eyes lit up and he rubbed his hands, for he had sworn to stretch upon his new war-drum the skin of the man who harassed him—and the drum's case had grown warped and cracked in the years of waiting.

"That is good talk," said a counsellor unfavourable to the king's white guest; "but it is well known that Sandi goes unharmed through terrible dangers because of M'shimba-M'shamba, the fearful spirit. They say that great regiments of devils march with him shrieking so that, where he has passed, the leopards lie dead with fright."

The old king was impressed, and licked the four fingers of his right hand so that no evil could touch him.

"Stuff!" said Joe loudly. "Ghosts—stuff! You'll get him good an' then these birds won't come stickin' their noses over the mountains no more. . . ."

The king listened, straining his neck towards the interpreter.

"Man, this shall be," he said, and Buliki was bidden to rise.

.   .   .   .   .

Just as the years of Old Egypt found themselves identified with the transient periods of kings, so was there a chronology of the river which has its significant association with a certain Lieutenant Tibbetts of the King's Houssas. Up at headquarters, the heads of little departments still speak of the Second Year of Bones as marking the process of a dynasty.

It was an *annus mirabilis* from causes which, in the main, had nothing whatever to do with Bones, as Hamilton of the Houssas had christened this lank subaltern.

Nor had it to do with the wonders which he worked by land and flood. Nor, exactly and truthfully, could it be said that he had any notable influence on the fecund soil which that year produced the most amazing of all harvests. Nor did he cause the river to overflow its banks (as it did) and wipe out thirty-five fishing villages and bring crocodiles ten miles into the forest where they fought in a beastly fashion with leopards and buffaloes.

Nor, and this must be placed to his credit and widely advertised, was he in the least degree responsible for the presence and personality of one who was flippantly described as "Lords."

New brooms may not always sweep clean, but, generally speaking, they raise enough dust to choke some men and bring tears to the eyes of others. Macalister Campbell-Cairns was the newest broom that was ever landed from a surf-boat to agitate the fever-bitten back-blocks,

and bring to the surface the murder urge which lies so
close to the skin of the most law-abiding.

This man was an Excellency, had on the lapel of his coat
miniature noughts and crosses that glittered at the end of
variegated ribbons; wore, as his right on such occasions,
a radiant paste star over his pancreas, and could put a
string of letters after his name as long as the name itself.
He fell from the surf-boat into the arms of a sergeant of
King's Houssas, fell from the tawdry little horse carriage
which brought him to Government House, into the
presence of a second and third secretary, a Chief Staff
Officer, and the Master of his Household; and eventually
fell into the thickly padded chair which was his by right of
his high office. And almost immediately the new broom
began to move around the dusty places, and there was
issued from Administrative Headquarters an Order of the
Day which was, to all intents and purposes, an Address of
Welcome to Sir Macalister Campbell-Cairns, written by
Sir Macalister Campbell-Cairns and signed in his indeci-
pherable hand. He had come (he said) to bring Light into
Dark Places; to do justice to white and black alike; to
offer an Inspiration and a Hope to the most Debased;
to establish Centralisation and curb the undesirable ten-
dencies of officials to usurp the functions of the Law. (He
did not exactly say this, but he meant this.) And last, but
not least, he Intended Making Himself Acquainted with
every Frontier Post of Civilisation for which he was
responsible. And if anybody had grievances would they
kindly keep them until he came along.

"O my God!" gasped thirty-three Commissioners, In-
spectors, Officers Commanding troops and the like when
this reached them.

Attached to the address of welcome was a "Very Secret
and Highly Confidential" note for the more important of
his subordinates.

*It has been brought to the Administrator's attention that
judgment of death is frequently given and executed by subordin-*

ate officials, particularly in the Reserved Territories. This practice must cease. All inquiries into cases of murder, treason, and incitement to rebellion must be remitted to A.H.Q., accompanied by a report of the evidence in triplicate, depositions (in duplicate) and a report of the findings of the court.

A month after this order was issued, Lieutenant Tibbetts, whose other name was Bones, chased a man who had murdered N'kema, the woodman, and stolen his wife, caught him on the borders of the old king's country, and hanged him within an hour of his arrest.

Thereupon was Hell let Loose at Administrative Headquarters, and the musical career of Lieutenant Tibbetts was threatened with extinguishment.

* * * * * *

Adolescence is a disorder which is marked by well-defined periods of fevers and flushings, shiverings of body and whizzings of head. Peculiar and symptomatic of these phases are strange cravings and aberrations, and a certain eccentric choice in the matter of condiment. For the bread of youth is better enjoyed when flavoured with an opsonium which is indigestible and even repulsive to the more educated taste.

The child who does not fix wistful eyes upon the cab of a railway engine is scarcely normal, the youth who has not envied the conductors of orchestras is hardly human. The young man who wishes that he could sit down at a piano and with an air of nonchalance run his fingers along the keys and dash straight away into the most complicated of musical compositions, has something wrong with him.

Bones had come to a state of development when he most passionately desired to make music. He had a portable harmonium in the corner of his hut and a viola under his bed. He could tell almost at a glance the difference between B flat and F sharp on any printed sheet. He had a small library on the Theory of Music, every book bound in royal blue with his monogram in gold on the covers. A trap drummer's outfit occupied a table usually and more properly reserved for the study of Cleary's Tactics and the Manual of Military Law.

Bones started his infamous musical career by the purchase of a clarinet—a long thing of wood and glittering metal. He bought this, as he bought most unnecessary things, because in the pages of his favourite magazine he had read an advertisement which told him to:

> *Learn to Play the Clarinet. Was Clerk, now Leader of Tawoomba Silver Band. Learning Clarinet Made This Man Owner of His Own House and Put $10,000.00 into Farmers Bank.*

"This man's" portrait was given to prove the *bona fides* of the claim. Bones thought $10,000.00 was ten millions, and sent 25 dollars by the next mail. He could never resist these bullying advertisements that order you to "fill up that coupon and send your money right away."

"I've got a soft heart, dear old officer," he apologised for the clarinet when eventually it came. "It's like drink to me, dear old captain. The minute I see one of those dashed old coupons I've got to sign it. I'm easily led, dear sir and brother officer—you can't drive old Bones. You can lead him but you can't drive him. That sort of thing runs in the family."

"Weak-minded?" suggested Hamilton.

"Not weak-minded—naughty, naughty!" Bones was waggishly reproachful.

"The point is this, Bones"—Captain Hamilton swung round in his chair and his eye was cold, his manner distinctly unfriendly—"I'm not going to allow you to learn to play that infernal instrument within five miles of the Residency."

"Ham, old sir," said Bones gently, "are you being just, dear old sir—justice, Ham, old superior, as jolly old Shakespeare says, blesses him or she who gives and him or she who takes."

Hamilton often blamed himself for his weakness in the matter of the clarinet. He should have put Bones under arrest or poisoned him or something.

Bones's love of music grew with what it fed upon. The harmonium was not a nuisance until he brought it into the open one warm night and played to 120 fascinated soldiers of the King's Houssas, their innumerable wives and progeny. The handbells (which marked the next stage of the disease) were a curse: twice Hamilton sprinted to the Residency, thinking he was late for lunch, only to discover that Bones was practising "Ring Out Wild Bells." Once the whole camp was turned out at midnight to catch Ali Ahmet's pet chimpanzee who had broken his chain and gone on a foraging expedition. It took three days to get him down from the high copal tree to which he had retired with a G major bell in one hand and the C sharp in the other, ringing them alternately day and night, with an expression of misery that was heart-breaking to witness.

The cornet which Bones had on approval from a trader at Sierra Leone was sent back by Sanders's orders as being demoralising to the armed forces of the Crown, for the first notes (as Bones played them) of "A Sailor's Life" so closely resembled the "Alarm and Assembly" call that headquarters was a constant ferment of armed men running to take up their positions.

"I have spoken to the Commissioner," said Hamilton, "and we have agreed that in future you will confine your musical exercises to a muted mouth-organ——"

"Very low, dear old officer," murmured Bones reproachfully. "Very *hoi polloi*, dear old sir."

"Or a jew's harp or a concertina." Then, seeing the eyes of Lieutenant Tibbetts light up; "A very small one—preferably rubber-tyred."

"He that hath no music in his jolly old soul," said Bones with dignity, "is fit for the jolly old ashpit."

"I shouldn't like to see you there," said Hamilton, "but I'm glad you're sensible of your limitations."

The tension of a very strained atmosphere was relieved by an order from Administrative Headquarters calling for the presence of the officer who carried out the execution of the old king's man. Bones was immensely interested.

"I knew something would come out of that, dear old sir," he said thoughtfully. "Mind you, dear old push-face——"

"Bones!" said his superior awfully.

"I mean I'm not going to accept any decoration, dear old sir," said Bones firmly. "I shall simply say to the jolly old Excellency: 'Sir, I appreciate the honour that the jolly old Government wishes to—er—bestow, and I deserve it. I did all the work, but whilst jolly old Ham hasn't a C.B. to his name——' "

"I don't wish you to talk about me at all," said Hamilton coldly. "And if you think you're going up to H.Q. to get bouquets, I'll tell you that the only flowers you're likely to get are those which will be handed to your next-of-kin. There's a kick coming. Haven't you seen the 'Private and Confidential'?"

Mr. Tibbetts's long face grew longer. He fixed his monocle in his eye and surveyed his chief sternly.

"If there is any kick coming, dear old superior—why me? Who was in charge on the Ochori? You, dear old Ham! Now don't try to get out of it. Uriah the Hitiddly-hi-ti did the same thing, and look what a horrible name he's got. As to that old order, I thought it was a joke——"

　　　.　　　　　.　　　　　.　　　　　.　　　　　.

　　　　　　.　　　　　.　　　　　.　　　　　　.

A visit to any Administrator is a solemn and unnerving business. To a new Administrator such a call is to be obeyed with trembling knees.

And Sir Macalister Campbell-Cairns was not only new but raw. They called him by various nicknames—an ominous sign. The man with one patronymic may be well loved; with two, well known; with half a dozen he is likely to be unpopular.

He had not occupied the chair of office longer than five minutes before he gave to the world his System of Responsible Control, which was roughly as follows: Every administrative unit was to be divided into as many districts as there were European officers. Each officer was to control a district and be responsible for its well-being and good conduct. The fact that he did not have his dwelling within 300 miles of the country made little or no difference. He might be a subaltern officer acting as tutor to wild Houssa men who were being moulded into military shape and learning for the first time that a rifle was not an instrument designed to frighten people to death, but an arm of precision which performed certain functions with mathematical exactness: that, in fact, the bullet and not the "bang!" was the real cause of all fatalities which followed its discharge.

Administrative Headquarters was the large name of a smallish town which was remarkable in that it boasted a municipality, a power plant, a waterworks and a reservoir in addition to a number of flat-roofed, whitewashed houses, built in gardens where only the more exotic flowers flourished. Horse-drawn street cars rattled along its boulevards; there were steam trains that ran at odd intervals into the jungle of the hinterland, and on the horns of the crescent-shaped water-front were two concrete forts which looked like inverted pill-boxes, but each of which accommodated a quick muzzle-loader and two 4·7 quick-firers of modern character.

In the main the population was made up of native ladies and gentlemen who wore respectively skirts and trousers. There were three churches to cater for the three degrees of Christianity which come to every native commune; the narrow and cheerless, the broad and cheerful, and the official brand which demands regular attendance on Sunday mornings and permits tennis and other decorous games for the rest of the day.

All commissioners hate A.H.Q., where natives speak English and are called "Mister" and wear frock-coats, stove-pipe hats and tight enamelled shoes on the Sabbath. The officers of the Territories regard a summons to attend at this unholy place with the same enthusiasm as the mother of a family might look upon an invitation to the White House if it was quarantined for measles.

Bones, who had no fear in his soul, journeyed coast-wise to headquarters, his mind entirely occupied by the new-born decision to discard all musical instruments in favour of the saxophone. Occasionally he gave a thought to the enraged Administrator.

Macalister believed in machine-guns, correspondence in triplicate, and confidence in the Man on the Spot. This latter belief originated when he found that he was the man. He hated all foreign wines and foreign dishes, had a passion for Scottish mutton and whisky, and possessed no faith whatever in the rising generation. When he was a boy, things were different. The people who went into the Diplomatic Service were gentlemen; women were modest and knew their place; children never spoke until they were spoken to.

He was a tallish, broadish man, with shoulders like an ox and a very red face that had seen a lot of hard wear. It appeared to have been originally modelled in red wax and to have been carelessly left in the sun.

"His Excellency will see you at once," said the third secretary, and looked at his watch. "You are ten minutes late." He shook his head.

"The boat was a day late, sir," said Bones.

The third secretary shook his head again, took off his white helmet and peered into its depths with half-closed eyes, his lips moving. He seemed to be praying. Then:

"This way, Mr. Tibbetts," he said, and walked rapidly down a corridor.

Bones, who had all a military gentleman's loathing and contempt for the Civil Service, followed at a slower pace to express his independence.

Sir Macalister was pacing up and down his large room, his hands clasped behind him, all the weight and burden of empire on his clouded brow. He shot a glance at the new-comer but did not pause in his exercise.

"Mr. Tibbetts, your Excellency," said the third secretary, in the tone of one who had caught the visitor after a hard chase.

"Huh," said his Excellency.

The secretary withdrew reluctantly: he would have liked to hear all that the Administrator had to say.

"So—you—are—Mr. Tibbetts!"

"Yes, sir."

"Your Excellency," snapped Sir Macalister. "No relation to the late—er—Sir John Tibbetts?"

"Yes, sir—my father."

"Oh!"

The Administrator was at a disadvantage: Sir John was the greatest official that had ever come to the coast.

"Indeed? Now, sir: will you tell me why—will you please tell me *why*, when you were policing the Chimbiri district, you *ex*-ecuted, without judge or jury, one Talaki? You will say that you were in a perilous position. You will say that you were five hundred miles from the nearest magistrate. You will say that you have precedents. You will say that the other miscreant escaped because you were understaffed." He stopped and glared at Bones.

"No, sir," said Bones politely. "None of these cute little ideas occurred to me."

"No, sir! Oh, indeed, sir! Now, sir—understand, sir! From this moment, sir!—and you may take this back to your Commissioner, sir! That no man is to die in his territories until his death warrant is signed and sealed, sir, by me, sir—the Administrator, sir! Or my authorised deputy, sir. Tell Mr. Sanders that, sir!"

Bones was not in any degree ruffled.

"Yes, sir," he said. "And when Mr. Sanders resigns, perhaps your Excellency will tell his successor?"

"Resigns?" Sir Macalister grew purple. Sanders was a tradition at the Foreign Office. The last time he resigned, a most important administrator was recalled. He was told when he reached home that it was so much easier to find a new administrator than a substitute for the Commissioner of the River Territories.

"Do you think he will resign, Mr. Tibbetts?" "Lords" was almost mild.

"Certain, sir: most unprofessional to send that kind of message by a jolly old subaltern." Bones shook his head reproachfully and added: "I might have to resign too."

The effect of this threat was not apparent. Bones afterwards said that Ruddy reeled. At any rate he resumed his walking.

"I'll go down and see him myself," he said. "It is shockingly unhealthy, but I must go. Why did you hang this fellow, sir?"

"Because, sir," said Bones, "he killed another fellow, sir, an' took his jolly old lady wife. . . ."

He explained how. Sir Macalister, who was not accustomed to the raw of life, shuddered and stopped him half-way through his narrative.

"Dreadful . . . you'd better come to dinner and talk it over, Tibbetts—seven-thirty sharp. Don't keep me waiting or I'll have you cashiered. And by the way, before I forget it, there is, I understand, some trouble in the old king's country. Ticklish business . . . wants tact. Tell Sanders I'll come down by the next boat and ask him to arrange a palaver with the old man. Eh? No, no, I shan't want Sanders there. I'll fix the boundary question—seven-thirty sharp, and if you're a minute late, by . . . I'll —I'll have you hoofed out of the Army, I will, by gad!"

Outside in the corridor Bones met a Sandhurst crony, one Stewart Clay—a child in white who wore the gold aiguilettes of an A.D.C. After the first whoop of joy and gladness:

"He's not a bad old devil," said the A.D.C. disloyally, "but he eats too much and drinks too much—especially drinks too much! When you hear him talking like a Dundee mill-hand, you'll know you have only to ask, to have. He's been crossed in love too," he added bitterly.

"Would you mind keeping off the subject of women, and especially Scottish women, to-night?"

Bones promised.

He came early and found Sir Macalister in the jocose or cocktail stage of affability. He even dared admit his purchase of a saxophone. The Administrator sneered at saxophones. Towards the end of dinner he confessed his own musical weakness.

"Mon," he said, "ye're daft if ye wouldna raither hear the bonnie pipies than ony flibberjigibbet of a saxophone! Stewart, laddie, gie me ma pipes oot of ma trunkie!"

When Sir Macalister talked this way he was happy: the stern Administrator had become the human Scotsman.

For two hours Bones sat in awe on the edge of his chair, his big hands on his knees, his monocle fixed, glaring respectfully at a big man in evening dress, his lapel glittering with decorations, who strode springily up and down the long dining-room, a tartan-covered bag under his arm, four beribboned pipes erect. . . . He played "Flowers of the Forest" and the "Lament of the Prince" . . . the pipes wailed eerily, dirgily but beautifully. And with his own administrative hands he put the bag beneath his guest's arm and taught him the strange, mad way of the bagpipes. Bones trod on air. . . .

"Ye're doin' fine! I'll gie ye an auld set I brocht oot for Stewart, but the laddie has nae gift for the pipes."

And, near midnight:

"Sit ye doon, Mr. Tibbetts. Ye'll be takin' the wee boat back to the Territories the morn? Aye—ye're young! Laddie, when I waur yere age I mind a wee bit lassie . . . Maggie Broon, by name. She waur a crofter's daughter, Tibbetts, she was no ma ain class, ye'll understaund. . . ."

Stewart Clay saw the visitor on his way to his hotel.

"He's not a bad old stick, but I wish Maggie Brown had died before he saw her. I get her two nights a week neat and undiluted!"

"Dear old Stewart," said Bones urgently, "which pipe

is it that you hang round your neck—is it the one that makes the ee-ing noise or the jolly old oo-er?"

Bones returned to his own headquarters a transfigured young man, and the engineer of the little *Bassam* was glad to see the back of him.

"I thought something had got into the guides, Mac," he said to the captain, "and there was me sluicin' oil into the dam' engine to stop the squeak, an' it was that herrin'-gutted officer-boy playin' on his so-and-so doodah all the something time!"

Sanders really did not mind—the presence of an Administrator in his area worried rather than awed him. He went down to the little concrete quay to say farewell to his Excellency, and since he had thoughtfully added certain comforts to the furnishings of the *Zaire* and reinforced the poverty-stricken cellar of the big white boat, Sir Macalister was almost friendly.

"Sorry to have given you so much trouble, Mr. Sanders," he said affably, "but I'm going to make this an annual visit . . . previous administrators have been a bit too slack."

"I should be very careful of the old king, sir, if I were you," said Sanders. "Personally, I should not have held the palaver—the mere fact that he asked for it so soon after the last little talk I had with his chief, looks very suspicious to me. You quite understand that this palaver was called by the king and not by me? He anticipated your message by twenty-four hours."

"So much the better, Mr. Sanders!" beamed his Excellency. "I shall find him in a conciliatory mood!"

The wheel of the *Zaire* began threshing astern. Bones, in spotless white, stood on the forward deck and saluted stiffly and magnificently, and the *Zaire*, backing slowly to midstream, turned her nose to the black waters and, her stern wheel whirling excitedly, she passed the bend of the river out of sight.

"I hope he drowns!" said Hamilton malignantly, as they walked back to the Residency. "And even drowning is too good for the man who introduced Bones to bag-pipes!"

But for once in his life Bones was content to leave the navigation of the boat in the capable hands of Yoka, who was chief engineer and shoal-smeller.

"I'm here if I'm wanted, sir an' Excellency," he explained gravely. "The mere fact that I'm standin' on this jolly old deck sort of gives the fellows confidence."

Sir Macalister, his sun helmet on the back of his head, paced up and down the awning-covered forebridge.

"You must tell me any places of interest we may pass, Mr. Tibbetts," were his only instructions, and Bones was talking for the rest of the day.

". . . that jolly old island there, dear sir, was where I fell out of a boat and was nearly swallowed by a naughty old crocodile . . . if you stand over here, dear old sir, you can see . . . no, you can't! . . . yes, you can! There it is . . . that village in the trees. . . . I was bitten by a shocking old mosquito and my jolly old arm swole—swoled—swelled up as big as your jolly old head . . . simply fearful! . . . You see that sandbank, sir, in the middle of the stream, sir? I was once stranded there for a whole day, sir . . . it was simply ghastly . . . nothing to see but water. . . . That village there, sir, is called . . . I'm dashed if I know what it's called." The listening Yoka supplied the name *sotto voce*. "Umbula . . . that's it—Umbula . . . rather like umbrella, what? haw, haw! That's not bad, dear old sir. . . ."

"Well, what happened in the village?"

"I was bitten by a dog there, sir . . . a jolly old cooking dog . . . simply terrible. . . . I had to stay in bed all day, sir. . . . That creek is called . . ." (Yoka obliged again.) "Libisini, that's it! It leads to a jolly old lake, sir, quite an extraordinary jolly old lake—all water and things. . . . I once fell into that jolly old lake . . . I got quite wet. . . ."

At the Ochori city Bosambo awaited his guests, and when he discovered that Sanders had not come his face fell.

"Lord, this is a bad palaver," he said, and for Bosambo

he was serious. "For my spies have brought word that two of the old king's regiments are sitting on the far side of the mountain. And because of this I have gathered all my spears and have sent throughout the land for my young fighting men."

Bones pulled at his long nose and pouted—sure evidence of his perturbation.

"Oh, ko! You tell me bad news," he said dismally, "for this man is a King's man and a very high One."

Bosambo surveyed the unconscious Macalister, busy at that moment, through his interpreter, in speaking to the headmen gathered to meet him.

"To me he looks like a fat cow," he said, without offence, "and this is a wonder to me, that all your high Ones are fat and old."

Bones was pardonably annoyed.

"You're a silly old josser," he said.

"Same like you, sah, and many times," returned Bosambo handsomely.

All that evening Bones spent in a vain endeavour to dissuade the great man from making the journey. They had with them an escort of twenty Houssas, and the road to the mountains led through dense thicket in which riflemen would be practically useless.

"Mr. Tibbetts," said his Excellency tremendously, "a British official never shirks his duty. That sacred word should be written in gold and placed above his head, so that sleeping or waking he can see it!"

"Personally, dear old sir," murmured Bones, "I never sleep with my jolly old eyes open. The point is, dear old Excellency——"

"Mr. Tibbetts, you are growing familiar," said Macalister.

Bones reasoned with the great man's A.D.C., and Lieutenant Stewart Clay gave him little comfort.

"He has no imagination," he said, "except about Scottish women named Brown. Give him another cocktail and see what that does."

Another cocktail produced in the Administrator nothing but a desire for music. Ten thousand Ochori warriors (for the city was now an armed camp) listened breathlessly to "The Campbells are Coming."

"Master," whispered the fascinated Bosambo, "why does the lord walk up and down when he makes those strange belly noises? Are there worse sounds yet to come?"

Later, when Bones produced his own gaily-ribboned pipes, Bosambo was answered.

At daybreak they started, ten Houssas and a hundred and fifty picked spears, and came to the foot of the mountain as the last rays of the sun fell athwart the low bush-trees.

"We'll rest here for an hour and finish the journey in the cool of night," said Sir Macalister, who had been carried the last twelve miles of the journey.

Bones wiped his hot and grimy forehead.

"Better wait till the morning, sir," he suggested. "The men are all in."

Sir Macalister smiled.

"Keep you fit, my boy," he said jovially. "I know the music to bring 'em along. You shall have a little practice, Tibbetts, my boy—ye're not pairfect yet."

In that great cleft of the Ghost Mountains which M'shimba-M'shamba had bitten in a night of terrible storm, a score of spears waited in the dark. The old king, wrapped in his rug of fur, crouched in the cover of the high cliffs, a hot bowl of glowing wood beneath his robe to give him warmth. Squatting at his feet, Joe the Trader sucked at a short, foul pipe.

". . . tell him that when this Sanders goes out he can go down into the Ochori when he dam' pleases. . . ."

One of the attendant counsellors had been lying flat and motionless on the rocky road, his ear pressed to the ground. Now he rose.

"They come," he said, and hissed.

The score of spears became a hundred. Form after form

flitted past, the waning moon reflected from their broad spear-blades . . . flitted past and disappeared. Hereabouts the ground is littered with boulders and there was cover for three men behind each.

"Let no man strike until they are a spear-length from me," coughed the king. "Sandi you shall bring me alive, also the young man with the silvery eye. . . ."

The counsellor by his side turned uneasily.

"If the terrible spirits come——" he began, and Joe recognised the words.

"Stuff!" he muttered. "Say, tell him he can have my skin if that happens . . . spirits! Come on, Sanders, you beauty!"

They heard the tramp of feet, caught fugitive glimpses of a swaying lantern. Behind the boulders men grew tense and gripped their killing spears hotly.

Out the of bush that encumbered the lower slopes of the big hill, the lantern came into uninterrupted view.

"Kill!" whispered the king.

But, even as he spoke, there came from the advancing column a strange and horrible sound. It was the shriek of a wounded soul—the scream of a man tortured beyond endurance—a savage and exultant howl amidst the fiendish titterings of ghouls. . . .

For a second the king stood erect, paralysed, his face working; and then, with screams of fear, the hidden spearsmen began to run, blinded by terror, throwing spear and shield as they fled.

"Tell him . . . only bagp——!"

Joe's words ended in a sob and he fell to his knees, striving vainly to draw out the spear that transfixed him; for the counsellor of the old king had struck as he ran.

*   *   *   *   *

"Yes, dear old sir," said Bones, as they tramped back to the Ochori city in the light of day; "terribly discourteous an' all that sort of thing. If a johnny makes an appointment a johnny ought to keep it."

"It was an ambush, by gad!" quivered his Excellency, bumping up and down as the palanquin-bearers negotiated a rough bit of track. "It is no use, my dear man, telling me that it wasn't an ambush . . . that horrible white man with the spear sticking in him! Good God . . . awful!"

"It may have been an ambush, dear old Excellency," admitted Bones; "but if it was, why did the jolly old sinners run away? That's what puzzles me."

And Bones was perfectly sincere.

III

THE VERY GOOD MAN

I

THE spectacle of a white man going native may be romantic—it is largely a question of locality and the imaginative faculties of his biographer. In the islands that stud the smiling seas, in a setting that may consist largely of smelly copra, but can as easily be "masked in" by garlands of frangipane, a man may take to himself an olive-skinned mama and excite no more than amused contempt amongst his decent fellows. But in Africa . . .

B'firi, the Christian woman, was young and comely. She had been the owner of three husbands, each of whom had loved her and died. After the third death the chief of her village held her for Sanders.

"It is not good that young men should die so quickly," he said at the palaver which followed; "and in the days of my father-his-father, this woman would have died for her witchcraft, for it is clear that she carries in her body a poison too strong for men. But now, lord Sandi, those good days are past, and we bring her to you that you may say wise words to her."

There was sarcasm here, but Sanders wisely overlooked the lapse. It was no more intricate or delicate a problem than hundreds of others which came to him for solution, but here he was relieved in his rôle of oracle.

The woman B'firi, silent till now, spoke:

"Lord, I am tired of men who never meet a good woman but they must have her better, and never walk with a bad woman but they leave her worse. I have spoken with the Jesus men on the Shagali river, and there I go to be washed in the river and wear cloth over my breast, for by this magic I will grow wings when I am old and live in the clouds with other ghosts."

This solved the problem, and B'firi went off, paddled by her two brothers to the Baptist Mission on the Shagali river (which was little more than a creek and was certainly not a river), and there she was baptised, learnt to make tea, "did" the lady missionaries' laundry, and acquired other Christian virtues.

She was clever. She learnt to speak English and read Bomongo in a year; at the end of eighteen months she was a lay preacher and went forth into the forest to carry the Word. Once, when she was conducting a mission of her own on the edge of the French Territory, there was a tremendous happening. A white man (sickly white he was) came swaying across the swamps. The people of the village called her, and she went out to meet him. His clothes were old and filthy, his solar hat was battered, brown, torn at the crown. She thought by the unsteadiness of his gait that he was drunk. He was. Behind him, at a respectful distance, walked his one carrier and servant, an elderly man of Angola, who supported on his head a large sugar-box containing the wealth and property of the unknown.

It did not need the influence of B'firi to procure him the shelter of a new hut. The man was white—not the browny-white of Sanders, but the white of trodden chalk.

In the morning B'firi with her own hands brewed him tea and carried the steaming bowl to his hut. The stranger sat up wild-eyed, glowered at her and took the tea from her hand.

"Where's this?" he asked huskily, between gulps. "What a filthy country! I wish I were dead! O God, I wish I were dead!"

She admonished him soberly—but in good English. The man blinked at her.

"What's this . . . missionary station? Thanks for the tea." He fell back to his pillow—a folded coat—with a shudder, and closed his eyes. When he opened them again she was still kneeling by the side of the skin bed, the bowl between her hands. He had once seen an ebony figure at Christie's like that—only that wasn't black. She did not wear the cloth which, wrapped tightly about a woman's body almost to the neck, proclaimed her Christian virtues. Only the little grass skirt, and all else of her was brown satin.

"Missionary, are you?" he asked weakly, when she explained her presence. "Try your hand on me! I've lost everything—everything! I gave up all that makes life worth while when I came to this blasted country—sorry."

She repeated the word with her lips: B'firi was what actors call a "quick study."

She understood men, having sapped three of their lives, and knew that they were happiest when they were talking about themselves. John Silwick Aliston was immensely sorry for himself—he pitied John Silwick Aliston with an intense pity that brought tears to his eyes. At the end of the fourth day of listening he came to the conclusion that she was a miracle sent to show him the way to salvation. She, bored to weariness, contemplated a magnificent future. The end of it all was that, when they came to the missionary station, he married this native woman B'firi— the missionary who performed the ceremony in proper style (B'firi being a baptised woman) was newly arrived from England, and had no definite views about the colour line. He believed that all humanity were God's creatures and that heaven was populated by beings of a neutral pigmentation. So he pronounced John Silwick Aliston, bachelor, and B'firi, pride of his mission, man and wife in the face of God and his congregation.

Mr. and Mrs. John Silwick Aliston went back to her father's hut, and the bridegroom drank three parts of a pint of forbidden rum and cried himself to sleep. For he was a Bachelor of Arts of Oxford University, and was absurdly conscious of his degradation—"absurdly," because he degraded his caste with open eyes.

Mr. Commissioner Sanders heard the shocking news

from one of his spies and flew a pigeon to Lieutenant Tibbetts, of the King's Houssas, who was fossicking round the Akasava country, looking for an Arab who had reputedly smuggled arms into the country.

Hoof Aliston out of country. Give hell missionary and report.

Bones made his way back to the big gas-launch that had brought him up-river, and three days later came up with the village where Mrs. Aliston was waiting for her husband to recover sufficiently from his attack of delirium tremens to begin her fourth honeymoon. Happily the missionary was away, and Bones was spared the most painful of his duties.

He found Aliston sitting before his hut, his head buried in his hand.

"Arise an' shine, dear old Aliston," said Bones. "Pine not, as the jolly old poet says, for partin' brings a nice kind of feelin'; let's say good-bye till we meet at Ealin'."

Aliston sprang up at the sound of a familiar tongue, and stood gaping at the unexpected apparition of a tall, thin, young man in a khaki shirt.

"Oh, sorry! Good morning," he said awkwardly.

"Pack up your dinky old traps, Aliston, dear old bird. Sunstroke very bad for you, sir an' wanderer. Fellows do things when they get a touch of jolly old Sol . . ."

Dimly the man began to understand.

"What is the idea, and who the devil are you?" he demanded resentfully.

"Deputy Commissioner, sir." Bones was very gentle. "Can't allow this sort of thing . . . good gracious! don't you know Kiplin'? 'White is white an' black is black, but they keep their own side of the street' an' all that——"

All that was masculine in John Aliston coalesced in a gesture of defiance.

"You won't think I'm rude if I tell you to mind your own business?" he asked.

"I shall, dear old Aliston—I certainly shall," proclaimed Bones. "I shall be simply fearfully upset. Get your kit, old sir."

Aliston stood squarely on his feet, his hands on his hips.

"I'm not going—and you can't force me."

A bony fist shot out suddenly and caught him under the jaw. The man sprawled down with a thud, and came whimpering and cursing to his feet. Twice Bones hit him before he fell and lay.

"Get up, silly old Aliston"; and, when he did not move, Bones stooped, gripped and brought him to his feet.

"You swine . . . !" sobbed John Silwick. "To hit a sick man . . . you brute!"

He went meekly enough between the two Houssas whom Bones's shrill whistle had brought to the spot.

Mrs. Aliston came flying through the village at the one end as her husband disappeared at the other.

"What is the meaning of this?" she demanded in a grey fury.

Bones answered her in the native tongue.

"Woman," he said, "this man belongs to my people, just as you belong to your people. There is the river and there is the land, and where they mix is mud and a stink."

"I am his wife," she answered tremulously, and there was murder in her eyes. "We are God-people and I have a book to show that I married in the God-man way. Also . . ."

She invented on the spur of the moment a very excellent reason for desiring her husband's companionship.

"I don't want to know anything private, dear old B'firi," said the agitated Bones very loudly.

She followed him down to the boat, arguing, pleading, threatening. Every dozen paces or so they stopped, Bones's long arms waving eloquently, Bones's thin shoulders shrugging with great rapidity. When the *Wiggle* cast off she took a canoe and six paddlers and followed him down the river. By the worst of luck the *Wiggle* struck a sandbank and grounded. She climbed aboard and was thrown into the river by the indignant soldiery, and, anchoring her canoe at the stern of the launch, refused to move.

In the short period of her new matrimonial experience, she had acquired vivid additions to her vocabulary.

Bones listened to her opinion of him for three seconds and then put his fingers to his ears.

"Naughty—naughty!" he roared. "You mustn't say that—you really mustn't . . . you won't go to heaven. . . ."

"____ ____ ____!" screamed Mrs. Aliston, employing one of her husband's most popular directions.

In the night, whilst she and her paddlers slept at the bottom of the canoe, one of the soldiers slipped overboard and towed her to the shore, fastening the grass rope with many knots, whilst his fellows, knee-deep on the shoal, pushed and shoved the *Wiggle* to deep water. In the morning, when she woke, the prison of her husband was gone and B'firi paddled back in fury to the mission station. Half-way she landed at a fishing village. The old chief of this was very rich, and all his wives wore big brass collars to testify to his affluence.

"If you come to my hut I will make you my chief wife and give you rings of brass for your legs as well," he said. "Also I will make you a fine new hut and my old wife shall be your servant."

B'firi pondered the matter.

"Will you become a Christian and let me wash you with water and say holy things to you?" she asked.

"One ju-ju is like another ju-ju," said the ancient philosopher, and Mrs. Aliston made her fifth marriage.

.   .   .   .   .

Sanders was on one side of his worn desk and a sullen, bearded man on the other.

"The point is, Mr. Aliston"—Sanders's voice on such occasions as these had the quality of an ice-cold razor—"that marriage in these territories cannot be performed between Europeans without a certificate issued by me.

Therefore your marriage was illegal in every sense. I feel that I should be wasting my time and yours if I attempted to bring home to you the foulness of these mixed marriages."

"It is a matter of opinion," growled the man, and then: "What are you going to do with me?"

"I'm sending you home as D.B.S. by the first available steamer," said Sanders.

The man went hot and red. His was the type of pride which revolted at being classified as a Distressed British Subject. Poverty with legitimate excuses he could confess. But to fix such a patch to the rags of his failure was intolerable.

The day the steamer called, he was missing. He had struck inland, and when they next heard of him he was teaching the interested Isisi the art of making mealie beer. Bones, with two trackers, went after him, but he had news of their coming. For three months they lost sight of him. Then Sanders, going up-river, was stopped in midstream by an old chief with a grievance.

"B'firi my wife has gone away into the forest with a white man," he quavered. "And, lord, she has taken a great collar of brass that is worth a hundred goats. . . ."

Sanders cursed under his breath and sent a pigeon back to headquarters.

This time Hamilton, with Bones and half a dozen Houssas, took up the trail, which led to the French border and the discovery of a new crime. An Arab trader had been attacked by a dozen lawless tribesmen led by a white. Four cases of gin had been stolen and a man killed.

Captain Hamilton did not stop to inquire into the presence of the gin-sellers so close to the forbidden area, but turned at right angles, and, late in the afternoon, came up with the camp of the robbers—nine stertorous and unconscious men and a dead woman; the long fingers of John Silwick Aliston were still about her throat when they found him, and Bones had to pry them loose.

"Poor old thing," said Bones in a hushed voice, as he looked down at the silent figure.

And then the glitter of something at her wrist caught his eye. It was a little golden bracelet, a cheap, hollow affair which had once held three small stones. One remained, a tiny, lustreless diamond. Stooping, he pressed the catch of the thing and drew it off.

"Humph!" said Hamilton, as he took the feather-weight trinket in his hand. "That little bracelet could tell a story, Bones." He turned it over on his palm. "American-made—five dollars net. How the devil did it get into the Akasava country?"

He handed the jewel back and Bones slipped it into his pocket. . . .

It was at three the following afternoon when Aliston became dimly aware of a life which was fast slipping from him.

"Hallo!" He looked up into the grave faces of the two officers. "Got me, eh? Where's B'firi?"

They did not answer.

"Hum . . . did I hurt her?"

The elder of the two men stooped and put something into his hand. It was a book.

"Prayer-book—what's the idea?"

Hamilton's eyes met his.

"In half an hour you hang," he said briefly. "Five of your friends have drunk themselves to death; the other two will go the same way as you. You don't want a judge and jury to try you, I suppose—with your name and filthy crime in the English papers?"

Chalk-faced, trembling, speechless, the man shook his head. They left him alone, but under their eyes, for the appointed time. One of the soldiers climbed a tree and fixed the rope, and then Bones walked to the man, who was squatting where they had left him, his head on his breast.

"Come," said Lieutenant Tibbetts tensely, and laid his hand on the shoulder of the doomed man.

With a scream, Aliston leapt up. For a second he stood swaying, and then stumbled and collapsed in a heap. He never regained consciousness, but died in the cool of the evening, and they buried him apart from the natives who swung from the trees.

2

It was generally agreed that Bones was not to be trusted alone. He was a good officer and a gallant fellow, but solitude and the absence of human props went straight to his head.

And he had been left practically alone on the station. Mr. Commissioner Sanders was up-country on his annual tax-collection, and Captain Hamilton was in bed with a very ordinary and conventional attack of malaria. It is true that he had the queer illusion that he was falling through the mattress of his bed right on to the spiky parts of the Albert Memorial, but that isn't really serious. People inured to malarial symptoms know that a case is only dangerous when the patient believes that he is Queen Victoria and that he is playing poker with Julius Cæsar for the fishing rights of the Rubicon.

Bones did not think his superior officer was in the slightest danger, nor did Sanders, nor did Hamilton, and the only wish that the sufferer had expressed was that Bones should refrain from nursing him.

It was unfortunate that the land wire which at odd periods connects the River Territories with Headquarters should have been repaired that week. The wire passes through the elephant country, and when the pachyderm isn't scratching himself against the wooden poles, he is pulling down the wire to discover whether it is good to eat. H.Q., in a burst of energy, had repaired it that week.

"O.K.?" asked H.Q.

Bones scribbled out a message and it was transmitted as spelt by the unimaginative half-caste telegraphist, who, to do him justice, thought he was sending a cipher message of the highest importance.

All well all well stop Comisoner at Ississi Isissi stop Hamulten sufering sevvere doze of marlarier but am carying caryrying carying on stop will do my best to save Hammilton life but feer feare fear the wost stop I will do my duty dutty.

Bones had an exasperating habit in all his written correspondence of spelling most words three times to discover which looked the most correct. If, as Sanders had so often pointed out to him, he had had the intelligence to cross out the two which found least favour in his eyes, his correspondence would have gained in clarity.

And then a great idea struck him. In case of serious sickness, Headquarters sometimes sent assistance. It was a privilege that Sanders claimed, and yet why not?

"Send good nurse," he added to the wire.

It looked lame. What Hamilton wanted was a motherly sort of woman . . . Bones added a technical adjective.

He stalked soberly back to the Residency, went into Hamilton's bedroom and laid a clammy hand on the brow of the sleeping officer.

"What (something violent) do you want, you (something worse)?" demanded the enraged invalid.

"Bones is here," murmured the visitor reassuringly. "Jolly old Florence Nightingale, dear old officer. Want anything, dear old Ham?"

"I want you to go to so-and-so out of here," cursed the sick man.

"Delirious! "murmured Bones, and tiptoed out, knocking over a table in his passage. "Tut, tut!" said the annoyed young man as the door slammed.

All that day and the greater part of the next he spent in devising little comforts for the invalid. Mama Pape, the Residency cook, watched the making of a jelly respectfully: Bones made it from a recipe he found in a cookery book. It was a pretty good jelly, but never quite reached the jelly stage.

"No, I *won't* drink it!" raved Hamilton. "I refuse to be poisoned . . . you made it? My ———!"

Cup and contents flew through the open window.

"Naughty, naughty," said Bones, in the tone of a mother to her child. "Let ickle Bones take um jolly old temperature."

Hamilton pointed a yellow hand to the door and glared fiendishly, and his attendant was hardly out of the room before he heard a bolt shot and the baleful voice of Hamilton hailed him.

"I've got an automatic and ten rounds here, and if you try to nurse me I'll blow the top of your head off."

"Dangerous," murmured Bones, and shrugged away his responsibility.

Left alone, the sick man swallowed three quinine tabloids, drank deeply of barley water, and went off into a healthy sleep.

The following afternoon, Bones was dozing noisily on the stoep of the Residency. The moving rays of the sun crept across the broad, white stoep and focused on the corn that decorated Lieutenant Tibbetts's little toe. He, too, dreamt. He was being burnt at the stake before Trinity College, Cambridge, for having spoken disrespectfully of the Jockey Club. The flames were licking his feet —especially one foot.

"Ouch!" said Bones painfully, and awoke to rub the outside of his mosquito boot tenderly.

And gradually, as he regained his faculties, he became aware of an extraordinary vision. There was sitting on a deck-chair, not half a dozen feet away from him, the most beautiful lady he had ever seen. She was young, and against the green of her helmet lining her hair shone like red gold. The lips that showed in the delicate face were almost a geranium red. They were curved now in a smile and the blue-grey eyes sparkled with laughter.

"Bless my jolly old soul!" murmured Bones, and allowed his long, lank body to subside into the chair again. "Bless my jolly old soul . . . shouldn't eat pork . . . phew!"

"Wake up, please!"

Bones opened one eye and saw all of her; opened the other and sat up, his jaw dropping.

"I've been sitting here patiently for a quarter of an hour," she said, and then, looking past her, he saw two large steamer trunks, a suit-case, a bag of golf clubs and a tennis racket.

"I'm the nurse from the Victoria Hospital," she said.

Bones staggered to his feet, uttering meaningless sounds.

"Bless my life and jolly old pants!" he gasped. "You're the young person . . . you're a bit young . . . how did you get here, dear old nurse?"

"By boat," she said. "I arrived by the *Pealego*."

"Come to nurse dear old Ham! Bless my life, what a peculiar thing!"

She stared at him.

"Ham—a man?"

Bones nodded.

"Fever?"

Bones nodded again, and she seemed relieved.

"He doesn't want nursing, dear old miss——" he began.

"Is he dead?" she asked callously.

Bones gaped, horrified—stared at her for a moment and dashed into the interior of the Residency. In ten seconds he leapt out again.

"No, young miss," he said, "he's alive. What I meant to say was that I'm nursing him my naughty old self."

She gazed at him solemnly.

"And he's alive," she said, half to herself.

Bones was hurt.

"And kickin'," he said reproachfully. "It may surprise you, dear old nursin' sister, but I'm a qualified nurse."

"You are?" She was, as he anticipated, surprised.

"I are, dear old red-cross one. I had ten lessons by correspondence. Symptoms, dear old nursing sister, are my speciality. I can tell at a glance——" He frowned at her critically. "You've got sunstroke—one eye's bigger than the other."

"It isn't!" she protested, pulled open the little bag she had on her lap, and drew out a very small mirror. "It isn't!" she said wrathfully. "They're both the same size. Where is the patient?"

Bones waved a large and sinewy hand to the door, fixed his monocle and looked serious.

"Treat him kindly," he begged. "In case of any relapse send for me, dear old Betsy Gamp . . . mind the mat . . . second door on the left. If he gets violent I'll come in with a jolly old mallet an' give him a sleeping draught."

He heard negotiations being conducted through Hamilton's closed door; heard the startled exclamation of his superior and the bolts pulled back.

"Who on earth sent for you, nurse?"

A low reply. Bones smiled complacently. He had accomplished something . . . he wondered if she played tennis or just owned a racket.

That evening he sat waiting for the nurse to make her appearance. It was within half an hour of dinner, and though he had caught a glimpse of her hurrying from the kitchen to the sick-room, the opportunities for conversation and exchange of confidences had not been offered. Every time he intercepted her she had some excuse for avoiding intellectual contact. The first time:

"I was goin' to say to you, dear old miss——"

She raised her finger to her lips.

"Hush!" she whispered. "He is asleep."

And the second time:

"I didn't ask you your name, dear old sister of mercy; you see, I'm in charge——"

Up went her warning hand.

"S-sh!" she breathed. "He is just waking up."

Bones was sitting, his gloomy mind fixed on the neglect he suffered, when he heard the puc-a-puc of the *Zaire's* stern wheel in the still night, and over the trees saw the haze of her smoke. In a second he was racing down the quay to meet the Commissioner.

"Yes . . . got back a week earlier than I expected—the

Akasava people are growing honest or else wanted me out of the country. How is Hamilton—I got your pigeon message—nothing serious, I hope?"

"No, sir," said Bones, and felt the moment opportune to announce the new arrival.

"A nurse?" repeated Sanders, amazed. "Why, in the name of heaven?"

Bones coughed.

"Dear old Ham has been pretty bad, sir," he said gravely. "Didn't even want to see me. When I peeked through his window, sir, he had his jolly old face to the wall, sir—so I sent for a nurse."

"Does it matter on what side a man sleeps?" asked Sanders innocently.

"Face to the jolly old wall, sir," murmured Bones, and shook his head. "That's one of the worst signs, sir, in the jolly old Pharmacœpia, sir. Face to the wall, sir . . . johnnies always pop off that way, sir."

"Stuff!" said Sanders, with the ghost of a smile. "Still, if the old lady is here we must make her comfortable."

Bones coughed again.

"Not old, sir, not so jolly old, sir. Rather on the young side, dear sir an' Excellency. Pretty, sir, in a way," he added daringly, and saw Sanders's face fall.

"It can't be helped—Hamilton will be all right. Headquarters are getting quite sprightly: as a rule they take a month to answer that kind of request."

He greeted the girl kindly—admired her in his detached way.

"I don't think I need stay very long." With a woman's instinct she guessed the reservations in his welcome. "Your Captain Hamilton isn't very ill. He is annoyed, but he is not ill."

She looked fixedly at Bones.

"Annoyance is illness," said Bones firmly. "A naughty temper is a sign of insanity, dear old hospital matron."

When the girl retired for the night, Sanders, who had had a chat with the sick man to discover the real cause of

his annoyance, took Bones out on the veranda and talked
to him gently.

"You must be awfully careful, Bones," he said. "I'm
afraid you sometimes use words which are just outside
the meaning you intend. For instance . . ." He gave an
instance.

"That means a motherly sort of lady, sir?" said Bones,
in astonishment. "Bless my life, sir . . ."

"Maternity nurse means something quite different,"
said Sanders, very steadily for a man who was shaking
with internal laughter. "And naturally Hamilton *is* a little
peevish. . . ."

Sanders employed the last morning of the girl's visit
showing her round the station. Her name was Rosalie
Marten, and she admitted her age as twenty-four.

"It must be lovely to be away from the natives in tall
hats and the electric light and cinemas," she said, drawing
a long breath. "I came out to West Africa thinking I
would have this kind of life—but Headquarters is a sort of
Clapham plus sunshine. There is no work I could do
here, Mr. Sanders?"

He shook his head.

"If it is not an impertinent question, Miss Marten, why
have you come to the coast at all? Have you friends
here——?"

"No," she answered shortly. "I hate the coast, that I
know: in some ways it is better than I thought it would be
—in most ways worse. I got my ideas from a trade newspaper that is run by a man who has never seen the other
side of the Sierra Leone mountain—my father is a
journalist and told me this. I hate the place—I hate it!"

The vehemence in her tone made him look at her
sharply, and looking, he guessed—a man. There was no
need to guess, for almost instantly she told.

"The man to whom I was engaged died here." She was
cruelly frank. "He came out two years ago."

Only for a moment did the voice lose control. Sanders
was silent. Such confidences as these almost hurt him.

The coast ate up these young lives ruthlessly, and this tragedy of hers had its duplicate.

"He was the very best man in the world—he came out to make sufficient money to buy a home. I am rather rich, Mr. Sanders, and he had to run the gauntlet of family suspicion. They thought he was a fortune-hunter—they told him this to his face, though I never knew this till afterwards."

"Was he . . . a missionary?"

She shook her head and smiled faintly.

"No . . . he was a very good man, but he was not a missionary. He died somewhere in the French Territory —he wrote to me soon after he arrived on the coast. It is terrible. . . ." She frowned. "Every day I pass the hotel where he stayed when he was in Headquarters. . . . I know the window of the room. He looked out of there upon the street along which I walk. It isn't believable, Mr. Sanders—it simply isn't believable!"

Sanders realised that she was talking as she had never talked to any human being. That she was expressing in words the long-inhibited confidence she had ached to give to somebody. He let her talk on without interruption as they slowly paced across the arid, dull ground.

"I've bored you awfully, but I feel better!" she said, half laughing, half crying. "I've often wished I were a Catholic so that I could confess to somebody. I suppose I shall recover in time and marry some poor man and put away my romance between sachets of lavender—hearts aren't easily broken."

When she went to her room, Sanders found an opportunity to utter a warning.

"'Ware light conversation dealing with death and destruction, you fellows," he said. "This poor girl has had a very unhappy experience."

It was no disloyalty to her confidence to outline the tragedy that shadowed this young life.

"We've got to be cautious an' entertainin', dear old sir and Excellency," said Bones, touched.

"For God's sake don't be that!"

Sanders and Hamilton spoke together.

"Maybe, insulting old superior, I could show her my curios?" suggested Bones, ruffled. "But of course, dear old sir, if you think the innocent old person would be corrupted——"

"I don't mind her being corrupted—I object to a guest being bored," said Hamilton.

"Get your curios, Bones," said Sanders good-humouredly, "but don't—er—enlarge on their history."

Bones sprinted to his hut and collected, hastily, the wherewithal of entertainment. Rosalie Marten came back to find three preternaturally solemn men who were galvanised at the sight of her into such a froth of artificial cheerfulness that she guessed the cause.

"You've been telling my sad story!" she said, almost flippantly. "I'm glad—but please don't be mysterious about it. I have an awful feeling that you are all on tenter-hooks for fear you hurt my feelings—please don't be tactful!"

Bones looked for a moment embarrassed, for he had arranged to be very tactful indeed. His pockets bulged with curios, gathered in the dark from the big box under his bed.

"We will be sorry to lose you, dear old miss," he said, when the strain which the effort of silence made had passed off and the Arab boy had handed round the coffee. "Three lumps or four? Bless my jolly old life, don't you take sugar? You'll never get as fat as podgy old Bones!"

"Mountainous is a better word," said Sanders.

"Which reminds me." Bones fumbled in his pocket. "This may cause you endless fun an' amusement, dear old hospital walker. It's the finger ring of the fattest man in the Territories—N'peru, the Akasava man. . . ."

He brought out a handful of miscellaneous oddments, wire bangles and anklets, carved wooden spoons, two strings of wooden beads, and a steel comb or two, and laid them on the table.

"This is a N'gombi woman's dinky little vanity bag——"

He heard her little scream and looked round in affright.

She had risen from the table and was staring at the little heap on the cloth. Her face was as white as death, and her trembling hand pointed at something.

"Where . . . where did you get that?"

She was pointing to a tarnished gold bracelet that had two stones missing.

"That . . . hum . . ." Bones for the moment forgot the injunction that had been served on him. "Well, to tell you the truth, young miss, that was taken——"

At that moment he caught Sanders's eyes, cold, prohibitive, and stopped.

"He . . . he had that," she said in a hushed voice, and picked up the jewel tenderly. "I bought it when I was a child . . . daddy took me to New York and I asked him to buy it. I gave it to . . . to my boy as a keepsake."

It was Sanders who found his voice first.

"What was the name of your—fiancé, Miss Marten?"

She was fondling the battered little bracelet, a smile of infinite fondness on her lips.

"John Silwick Aliston," she breathed. "The best, the dearest man in the world."

A silence so profound that she could have heard the deep breathing of the men, were she not so absorbed in the pitiful relic she held in her hand.

"A very good chap, one of the best." Bones leapt into the breach. His voice was husky and he spoke in a jerky, breathless way. "Dear old John—what a lad!"

She looked up at him quickly: the two men found breathing difficult.

"You knew him?"

Bones nodded; his blazing eyes held the light of inspiration.

"Rather, dear old nurse. Met him up on the French border . . . real good fellow . . . fever. . . ."

"You were with him when he died?"

Bones's head went up and down like an automaton.

"Yes—cheerful to the last—brave old fellow—full of pluck, dear old miss. Gave me this bracelet for his girl—never told me her jolly old name, though. One of the best, dear old John——"

He stopped, exhausted by his effort.

She looked for a long time at the trinket, then held out her hand.

"Thank you," she said in a low voice. "I shall always think of you. I am sure you were good to him—God bless you!"

Bones could have wept.

IV

WOMEN WILL TALK

IF you hack down a copal tree and let it lie in a high place where the sun can warm it and the rain cannot rot, and, when it is duly seasoned, you cut a three-yard length of it and with great patience carve out its middle from one end, you have an instrument of communication which was ancient when the French revolutionaries were experimenting with the semaphore, and was effective in the days of the Cæsars.

M'gliki, the *lokali* man of the Akasava city, was very, very old and nearly blind, so that he stumbled about, up-setting cook-pots and breaking rare clay vessels, and this was a family scandal because, by law, the family connections of silly people are responsible for the damage they do in their foolishness.

Yet, old and fumbling as he was, there was no man in all the world (which stretches from the Ghost Mountains to the River With One Bank that we call the sea) could play upon the hollow tree-trunk like M'gliki. Seated before the battered trunk and wielding two heavy sticks, he sent forth his rolling, rataplanning messages, the gossip of the city, urgent calls to far away fishermen, personal messages from family to family, tales of death and birth, of marriage and newly discovered scandal. Every flourish, every cadence of the *lokali*, that most wonderful signal drum, has its significance. Sanders of the river could read M'gliki's messages thirty miles away on a still night, for the old man never made an error.

"Long roll . . . short roll . . . long roll . . ."

That was Sanders by name: a little "tune" that followed meant going south; three sharp taps on the end of it was the equivalent of "no complaints." Sanders got to recognise the name of every chief and tribe that the drummer tapped forth. Could read warning and promise, tale of theft or murder.

All day long the old man sat before his wooden drum staring with unseeing eyes across the broad river. When the rains came they built a little shelter for him, otherwise he would have stumbled back to his hut and broken more pots that the family must pay for.

After a particularly disastrous evening, when M'gliki had trodden on the hafts of three new spears, had over-turned a pot of fish and half killed a valuable cooking dog, his eldest son and his youngest brother had a secret conference.

"Let us go hunting in the Forest of the Little People," said the son, "and we will take M'gliki with us, saying that we need him. And when we are there and he sleeps, we will go away and leave him, and, being an old man and blind, he will soon die."

The son and the brother took away their relative one morning and paddled for five days until they came to the Dark Woods. M'gliki sat at the bow, with a tiny but sonorous little *lokali*, and his drum rolled all the way, telling the world that he was M'gliki, the famed *lokali* man, and that these with him were his fine strong son and his own brother.

In the forest they slept one night, and, hiding the small *lokali*, they slipped away in the light of the moon, leaving an old man to face the fierce little bush people and the yellow-eyed leopards that slunk from tree to tree in a wide circle about him.

And here he might have died, but a little girl found him and led him to a place of ten huts (which is a large village in the bush sense). Her name was Asabo, and she was very ugly even at the age of seven. Her father was the first man of the village, and when he had overcome his natural desire to try the effect of a new poison with which he had tipped his arrow-head upon the unsuspecting visitor, he gave him a corner of his hut. And from then onward the bush people possessed a new asset, for

M'gliki spent his days teaching Asabo the wonder. The small *lokali* had been found hidden under a tree, and, to the wonder of the village, Asabo progressed in wisdom.

"You shall be the greatest woman in the world," prophesied M'gliki. "You shall marry a chief and sleep on a skin bed; also you will have three lovers, who will come to you at different times, and none shall know the other, and your husband shall know none."

Asabo made a hoarse noise of pleasure, for when this prophecy was made she was ten and soon was to meet the Supreme *Ouda*.

Now and again to all races comes a being of super intelligence whose personality dominates his fellows. These creatures are born at rare intervals and their influence runs beyond their own tribes. A play-acting Shakespeare, a versatile Leonardo, a brandy-inspired Peter Romanoff, a vision-seeing Mahomet, these magnetic mountains come smoking up in divers seas and set the compasses of mariners quivering to new northings.

Mr. Commissioner Sanders had a large number of native agents who kept him in touch with events of interest to himself and his Government. These spies of his formed so competent an intelligence service that at any moment he could have given a rough survey of the social and economic conditions of every one of the twenty-three tribal communities it was his job to govern. From one area alone news was fragmentary and unreliable. In the deep forest of the Iguri dwelt the Little Hunters, a shy and savage people who brooked no interference and resented attention. A normal-sized spy, in a land where the average height of the people is thirty-eight inches, is necessarily a conspicuous figure.

Sanders had held palavers on the edge of the forest with a tiny, pot-bellied headman, and had secured a promise of annual tribute in the shape of skins, rubber and gum copal; and this yearly contribution to the funds of government had been made regularly. Year after year, in the month of the New Green, the little *Wiggle* had chuffed up the long, narrow river which runs to the border of the Iguri forest and had found, in a clearing, an odd collection of rubber and gum piled up on one side of the landing-place and a stack of dried skins on the other. Generally there were in attendance two ferocious little men, who beat a retreat at the first sight of the launch and watched the transfer of the taxes from a respectable distance.

There came a day when the launch was to find nothing —neither skins, nor gum, rubber nor men.

.   .   .   .   .   .

The hour was near midnight. Sanders had gone to bed, but one of the two young men who played picquet under the light of the oil lamp had no appreciation of time.

"That rubicons you, Bones," said Captain Hamilton complacently, as he totted up the score.

Mr. Tibbetts's face was a mask.

"We'll have another game, dear old Ham," he said; "but, dear old officer, do you mind turnin' up your sleeves before we start?"

"What the devil do you mean, Bones?" demanded his superior hotly.

"Nothin', sir; a mere matter of precaution, dear old captain. You've held all the kings an' aces since ten o'clock. Play fair, dear old sir—all that I ask is that you turn up your sleeves."

Hamilton transfixed him with a cold-light glare and dealt the cards. It was annoying that Bones fixed his monocle firmly in his eye and kept his gaze glued on the dealer's hands, and not remarkable in consequence that Captain Hamilton bungled the deal and gave himself one card too many.

"Ah!" said Bones significantly. "Pick the cards you want—don't mind me."

"Bones! You're insulting!" stormed the other.

Bones gathered up his cards with a meaning smile.

"I've got an ace, dear old manipulator!" he said, in

mock concern. "Some mistake here, dear old Ham—
would you like a fresh deal?"

Hamilton said nothing—he scored a hundred and forty
and capotted his opponent, who had misguidedly dis-
carded his ace.

"Shall I deal?" asked Bones politely.

"If you please." Hamilton was very short.

"I say nothing, dear old officer and gentleman, but I
think a lot," said Bones, as he took up his hand.

"I've never noticed it," said Hamilton.

When it came to his turn to deal, he had to ignore the
spectacle of Bones popping his head down to look under
the table, and pretended that he did not see his unspeak-
able companion feeling the backs of the cards for secret
marks.

"Luck is luck, dear sir and brother officer," said Bones,
examining his cards; "an' play is play. But dealin's got
everything skinned to death." He frowned at the cards.
"Excuse me, dear old Ham, but this doesn't look like the
same pack——"

Hamilton flung down his cards.

"Bones!" he hissed. "If you suggest that I'm cheating
I'll break your infernal head."

"It will be the only part of me that's not broke, Ham,
old light-fingers," said Bones. "I've lost nearly four
shillings in three hours!"

"Which you'll never pay," said Hamilton fiercely, as he
got up. "Bones! You're impossible. You will parade your
platoon at 7 a.m. and put them through physical drill."

"Dirty work!" murmured Bones. "The man not only
ruins me but lets his naughty old temper get the better of
him. Uses his dashed old superiority to make me a jolly
old gallery slave. You're worse than Uriah the wicked old
Hittite. See Bible."

The next morning Sanders came out of his little office
looking unusually serious. He held between finger and
thumb a cigarette-paper covered with fine Arabic writing.
Hamilton saw the paper.

"Pigeon?" he asked. "You were up early, sir."

Sanders walked to the sideboard, turned the tap of the coffee-urn and brought his steaming cup to the table.

"The sergeant of the guard brought the paper at daybreak," he said. "The little fellow had a hawk on his tail and was lucky to get here. Where is Bones?"

Hamilton screwed his head sideways: through the open door he commanded a view of the parade ground, where a squad of twenty men were engaged in the military exercise which has come to be called "physical jerks." Lieutenant Tibbetts, in white duck trousers, sports shirt and helmet, was in command, and his raucous, squeaky voice came to them. His language was a curious mixture of coast Arabic, Bomongo and English.

"O sons of awkward parents, is it thus I taught thee? You silly old jossers! When I say 'one,' put both hands upon thy loins and bend thy knees. Not as old women with creakings and groanings, but like young antelopes. Dash you, Abdul, keep still, you fidgety old blighter. Now sink to thy heels, keeping thy belly—oh, ko! Man, you are like a blithering old cow! Get up! Go down!..."

"Bones seems to be busy," said Sanders.

"Bones has to be disciplined," replied Hamilton primly. "He must occasionally be put in his place. I cannot allow Bones to describe me as a card-sharp and retain my self-respect. I played picquet with him last night, and I admit the cards ran badly for him. When he asked me to turn up my sleeves, I felt that he was going very far, but when——"

He described what had happened; and although Sanders never felt less like laughing, he chuckled.

"I was very annoyed indeed with Bones," said Hamilton, but he was grinning.

The object of his annoyance came in to breakfast soon after, and Bones was stiff, not to say distant.

"'Morning, Bones." Hamilton was in a conciliatory mood.

"'Morning, sir." Bones saluted regimentally. "Parade dismissed, sir."

"Come down off that horse of yours, Bones—you *were* insulting. Admit it."

Bones, with a cup in one hand, saluted again with the other.

"Any complaints you have, sir, should be reported to the jolly old commander-in-chief. I'll be glad to answer any letter you send to me, but, if you will excuse me, sir, we will not exchange badinage or saucy quips, sir."

"Bones, I want you to go up to the Iguri forest and collect the Bushies' taxes."

Sanders broke in upon the chilly atmosphere.

"You may take the *Wiggle*, but you are not to land. If the bush people are normal I would like you to see their chief, but particularly I wish you to make contact with a man named K'belu. Avoid trouble—there may be quite a lot coming our way—but above all, keep your maxims in working order until you are clear of the bush country."

"It's quite on the cards——" began Hamilton, but his subaltern silenced him with a gesture.

"Keep off your favourite vice, dear old sir," he said haughtily. "And anyway, I've finished gamblin'."

"I'm not so sure that you have," said Sanders quietly. "I shall be glad when you have returned—with or without the taxes."

. . . . . .

In the deeps of the great forest there had been born *cala cala*, a tiny little grey-brown animal whom its parents had called K'belu, the Brown Mouse. The place of his birth was a nest between the forks of an enormous oak, for his kind were the lowest type of pygmy people and his parents lived alone in the forest. Such was the immense spread of the fork that the floor of the hut was even and the grass-woven walls and roof combined with the protection afforded by the spread of the boughs to make the place watertight. And here he grew and thought, was fed and beaten, learnt the poisonous properties of plants and a certain strange caterpillar; and in due course accompanied his tiny father on his hunting expeditions.

There was an enterprising missionary in the Iguri who had spent his life in the study of bush people, first in Central-South and now in Central-West Africa. He loved the bushmen because he believed that they were the first men in the world; and K'belu made his acquaintance at an early stage of his existence. The God-man had a house on the edge of the forest, where he grew bananas for the bushmen to steal. Even when they discovered that they could have the fruit for the asking, they continued to steal —this process of acquisition being less embarrassing than any other. One day the God-man, whose name was Father Matthew, caught K'belu in the act and chased him with surprising agility, remembering that he was a fat man and encumbered with the long, brown habit of his order. He did not kill K'belu, or pick out his eye, or bite at his heart, or do any of the things which missionaries are supposed to do. He took the squirming child back to his garden, gave him a dish of goat's milk and as many bananas as he could carry. After, when the child came (timidly and suspiciously at first), he showed him certain devil marks, such as A and B and C.

At the age of ten K'belu could read Bomongo, which is the language of the forest, larded with certain ancient words which are the pygmy's very own.

Soon after this the missionary died of some obscure tropical disease, and on the night of his death K'belu went to his house and stole all the books he could gather and carried them away to his hut. When his father died, at the ripe old age of thirty-six, the boy went into the nearest village, carrying his father's arrows and his treasure. The chief of this tiny community gave him a hut in exchange for the arrows.

And then, when the superiority of the newcomer was forced upon him (for did he not read books full of devil marks, like Father Matthew himself?), he took counsel with his wife and went to the hut of his guest.

"I see you," he said, as he squatted down, and came at once to the point. "I have a daughter, and she is a wonderful woman, making strange noises on a tree trunk, as she was taught by M'gliki, the N'gombi man who died of the sickness when the river was in flood and the woods were full of fish. I will give this woman to you for ten arrows and as much salt as a man can hold in two hands."

"Arrows I have none, nor salt," said K'belu loftily; "but I will take this woman from you because I am a man with a wish for children."

He was fifteen and of a marriageable age, and after some demur the father agreed and paid for the feast that constituted the wedding.

Thereafter Asabo dwelt in the hut of her master, worked for him and absorbed his mystery—for all day long he thought and thought. There was at the back of his mind an idea, dimly seen at moments, never wholly comprehended. They saw him poring over dog-eared books, and the word went through the forest that K'belu was *Ouda* and a man to be propitiated. Now *Ouda* is the devil of the pygmy people, a worker of mischief and yet a giver of gifts—the only deity they know.

His fame grew, and the idea became concrete. One day he summoned a palaver of all people, and none questioned his right, for the pygmies are a loose-knit democracy, without chiefs in the literal sense.

"All men listen to me," said K'belu. "I have learnt by my magic that we are the high lords of the world because of our smallness. What men can climb as we? What men can swing from branch to branch? Who are feared as we? None in the world, because we are the masters of all people, who are our slaves."

The little folk listened and wondered whilst the Idea found exposition.

"Head of every tribe of the outer people," said K'belu, "was a chief. Above them was Sandi and his two sons. If the chiefs died and Sandi died, who would be master of the world? Surely their killers? And if new chiefs rose and a new Sandi came with his sons (the whole Territory insisted upon this relationship of Bones and Hamilton) they also would die until the omnipotent They who sent these white men to give the law would weary of their effort and the land would be left to the cunning little people."

It seemed a good idea. Three thousand bushmen began to grow conscious of nationality.

"In a moon and the rind of a moon Sandi will come to rob us of our gum and rubber and the little skins of monkeys. Or his son with the silver eye, or the man with the loud voice who shouts at the soldiers" (this was a libel on Hamilton). "But I, K'belu, the *Ouda* of the people, say that we will give him only the gum of caterpillars."

His words had been heard in silence, but now an important man from the Dark Woods spoke:

"This is good talk, K'belu, but if Sandi comes with his little gun that says 'ha-ha-ha!' there will be an end to us."

He finished his words and fell forward, his breast on his knees; for K'belu, expecting opposition from this man, had stationed a creature of his in a tree, and at his signal a bow twanged behind him and the arrow-head came redly out of his breast. There was no further opposition.

K'belu went back and told his wife.

"O K'belu, I see that you are *Ouda*, and a very great lord. And when you are king of the world I will wear beautiful brass anklets and sleep on a skin bed."

She said nothing about the unfulfilled prophecy about the three lovers. They would arrive as a matter of course. In her joy and exhilaration she kept the village awake half the night. Through the dark hours her *lokali* rattled and droned the song of her triumph.

For the first time in all probability since the days of the Egyptian dynasties, the bush-folk enjoyed a leadership. K'belu's first act was to round up the unsociable units that lived in the forest alone and combine them into villages. The little men hated this interference with their liberty—

they are the freest people in the world, and in consequence
the most degraded—their wives made throaty noises of
protest, their eighteen-inch sons and daughters trudged
at their heels into the new compounds with a lively sense
of excitement to come.

In the midst of the greatest of the villages, K'belu set up
a palace of grass, and here he met his awkward counsellors, who had never before engaged in communal activi-
ties. And so matters went till, on the wane of the second
moon, came Bones, cautiously, to the spot appointed for
the collection of taxes.

The *Wiggle* hung around for the best part of a week, and
then Lieutenant Tibbetts sent a native into the forest to
make inquiries. This messenger was a man of the Isisi,
who knew the bushmen and spoke their queer language.
Three days passed and then, in the middle of the night, a
Houssa soldier woke Bones.

"Master, I have heard strange sounds on the land near
this little ship," he said.

Bones pulled his pliant mosquito-boots over his
pyjamas and went out on the deck to listen. It was a wind-
less night of stars and there was no sound but the lap-lap
of water against the boat side. No bird's hoarse note
broke the stillness. A leisurely meteor streaked whitely
across the sky.

"What were the sounds, man?" he whispered.

"The sound of men walking and the dropping of something on the ground," was the reply.

Bones bent his head, listening. He heard a gurgle in the
water; that was a crocodile swimming past . . . nothing
more.

It was nearly five o'clock. The launch was moored to
two gum trees, and the moving chains were paid out at
nightfall so that there was a dozen feet between shore and
boat, a position made possible by the conformation of the
river's bank, for the drive of the current caught the *Wiggle*
broadside on end; had the cables parted, she would have
been pushed to the opposite bank.

Bones went back into his cabin, slipped on an overcoat, found his electric torch, and took his automatic from under his pillow. The bow of the boat was nearest the shore, and he moved noiselessly forward till he stood against the little windlass to which the mooring rope was reeved.

Then, suddenly pressing the button of the torch, he shot a beam of white light towards the bank. The light followed the direction of the taut cable, and the first thing he saw was a monkey-like figure coming hand over hand along the wire rope. Beyond, the bank was crowded with tiny, naked figures.

Out went his light instantly and he dropped to the cover of the gunwale—and not too soon.

"Tap . . . tap . . . tap!"

A sound like the patter of hail. Bones waited until the first shower of poisoned arrows had fallen, then, jerking his Browning over the gunwale, he pumped ten shots into the midst of them.

"Cover!" he roared as he heard the sleepy Houssas scrambling from their blankets.

But no other arrow fell, nor did he expect a second shower. By this time the brown horde was flying to the cover of the woods. They never attacked in the face of firearms.

Daylight came suddenly: a faint paling of the east that showed the motionless silhouettes of the big copal trees, a sudden pandemonium of sound as if a million birds had begun twittering at once, the mumbling chatter of monkeys, and the world was light and all the tree-tops were gilded in the first rays of the sun.

"Dear me!" said Bones.

Within a dozen yards of the river's edge a rough pole had been planted, and tied thereto was the native whom he had sent into the forest. At least, Bones guessed it was he: he was rather difficult to recognise.

He stared for a long time at the dreadful thing and gave the order to warp the boat to the bank. The machine-guns fore and aft swung over to cover the dark trees behind which the little brown men were lurking.

"Take a crew ashore, Ahmet, and let them bury the man."

Bones watched the quick work from behind the fore Maxim, his eyes roving between the working party and the wood. When all was done and the men had washed themselves in the stream:

"Cast off the big ropes," he said in the vernacular.

The danger was by no means over. Before they reached the main river, the stream passed for two miles through the heart of the forest. The tributary ran between high banks not twenty yards apart, and here the trees came down to the very edge of the water, a heaven-planned site for an ambush. Moreover, a tree hastily felled would block his exit. Turning the nose of the *Wiggle* downstream, he took his place at the wheel.

"Let all men take cover," he ordered, and, when this was obeyed, he drove the boat forward at full speed.

Yoka, the steersman, alone remained with him.

"Go, man," said Bones sternly.

"Lord, this is death," said the stout Yoka, "for the little men will be waiting in the Narrow Place and——"

Bones snarled round on him.

"Go to cover or I will whip you till you bleed," he barked.

Yoka went reluctantly.

An hour's run through open country and the woods loomed ahead. There was no sign of a blockade—the woods were lifeless, but he saw birds circling round the tree-tops in an aimless, excited way, and knew that they had been disturbed.

Locking the wheel, he slowed, and, diving into his cabin, brought out his dingy eiderdown quilt. Hanging this loosely over his head, he sent the boat at top speed for the narrow lane of water. Presently he was in the wood and darkness fell, for the trees form a green roof to the river.

Bump!

He had grazed the slope of a little sandbank and the launch veered and slithered until it was under the high bank. This accident gave him an idea. He kept the *Wiggle* as near to the dangerous bank as he could. The little men would be reluctant to leave cover. . . .

Two hundred yards ahead of him, he saw a big tree lying over at a suspicious angle and drooping slowly. Somebody was hacking furiously at the trunk . . . if it fell, its great branches would offer a barrier not to be penetrated. Bones watched, fascinated, forgetful of his own danger, till the first arrow struck a spoke of the steering wheel and went humming past his head at a tangent. He felt the smack of another as it struck the quilt, ripping the faded silk into slithers.

The tree was leaning drunkenly . . . he shot under it as it fell and heard the rustle and crackle of twigs as they struck the stern of the boat.

"Phew!" said Bones, as the trees began to thin. He threw aside the hot quilt. "Confound their little whiskers!"

He was wet through, limp. He had gripped the wheel with such a fierce intensity that the palms of his hands were blistered.

"O Yoka," he called, and, when Yoka came: "Bring me," said Bones, in the Arabic of the coast, "a dish of nectar such as the lily-eyed houris of Paradise pour from vessels of gold."

"Lord," said the puzzled Yoka, "does your lordship mean whisky-soda?"

"A double one," said Bones, and smacked his dry lips.

His triumph died in his throat.

Ahead, as the steamer turned a sharp bend of the river, he saw an isolated tree topple over and fall into the water with a mighty splash, and at that second the wood was alive with the little men, and the arrows came towards him in shoals.

Bones reversed his engine instantly, but it was an

eternity before he moved astern. The pygmies had broken from cover and were racing along the wooded bank. Death was before and behind, and though as yet the arrows fell short, they would reach him sooner or later.

Leaving the wheel to Yoka, he sat down to the machine-gun and in a second the wood re-echoed to its staccato notes. As if by magic, the little people disappeared at the first shot. He stopped the engine and slowly the launch drifted back to where the larger part of his enemy was waiting. He surveyed the obstruction with a sinking heart. The *Zaire* would have broken through it, but he had a fifty-foot launch that would buckle up at the first impact.

The arrows were still pouring down into the water; one struck the bow . . . in a very short time they would reach the deck.

He turned, ran into his cabin and scrawled a message on a thin sheet of rice-paper. Yoka brought him the pigeon, and the dispatch was fastened to the red leg with a rubber band.

"Home you go, you lucky old coo-er," said Bones, "an' I wish I was comin' with you."

He flew the pigeon and watched it circle and then, as the boat drifted into the bank, slipped four loaded magazines into his pocket, two for each pistol, as the first of the bushmen dropped to the deck. . . .

"Let all these men be brought to me alive," had been K'belu's order, "especially the young man with the shining eye who is the son of Sandi."

Miraculously, only one of the party was killed in that final rush of the little men, and Bones marched through the forest at the head of a dejected escort. That night he was brought before the *Ouda*.

"I see you, son of Sandi," said K'belu. "Now you know that we are a great people, for we have overcome your guns that say 'ha-ha-ha' and your terrible soldiers."

He was extremely ugly, but not quite as ugly as the undressed little woman who danced by his side, snapping her stubby little fingers in an ecstasy of joy. For now the fine skin bed was very near at hand and the first of the lovers had looked at her meaningly.

"O fool!" said Bones. "Where are they who have stood up against government? Do they not hang upon a tree until their bones slip through the rope? Sandi will hear and he will come and you will go to the place where the shadows of monkeys live."

"Eat his heart!" screamed Asabo, prancing frantically. "Give me this high man and I will make him into three little people."

Her husband pushed her aside ungently.

"Sandi will never know," he said, and then he heard a wild squeak of fear, and the great crowd that surrounded them began to melt until only the prisoners, K'belu and his wife remained. Yet there was nothing to be seen, for the Houssas who were coming through the forest had painted their bayonets black that they might not reflect the light, and Sanders wore a dark coat over his khaki and was bareheaded. Even Bones did not see him till he came into the light of the fire.

"O K'belu!" said Sanders, and the little bushman made a grimace.

"First you will kill Tibbetti and then this chief and that, and lastly you will kill me," said Sanders with his cold smile. "Little man, what do you say that you do not die this night?"

Presently K'belu found his voice.

"Lord, how did you know these mysteries?" he asked.

"Women will talk," said Sanders cryptically, and looked round for the *lokali* that Asabo had rattled so joyously, sending out to the world the story of her husband's greatness.

. . . .

"Fortunately," said Sanders, as the *Zaire* went swiftly down the big river, "Asabo's message was relayed. Ahmet in the Isisi heard it and flew a pigeon, but I knew before. Hamilton wanted to come—but somebody had to stay behind."

"Yes, sir," said Bones, with the memory of his griev-ance still upon him, "to put the jolly old cards in order."

V

THE SAINT

From time to time there passed through Sanders's head-quarters men and women who had devoted their lives to the well-being of native people. Sanders did not share the prejudice against missionaries common in Government circles; on the other hand he did not favour them, because they established, unconsciously, a new authority.

"Lord," a new convert once asked him, "there is a new master here called Jesu-God, and if we do things that please Him we need not do things which please your lordship."

"O man," said Sanders, "if you do not please me, you do not please Him, and I will come with my soldiers and you will be sorry, for He is my own God and I have known Him longer than you."

An outrageous claim by every ethical test, but in the black lands which Sanders governed, eight hundred words form an extensive vocabulary, and there is no scope for the finer shades of definition.

Mrs. Albert arrived one morning, and was not unexpected. Headquarters had forwarded a massive documentation concerning the lady; she was the daughter of a peer of the realm, the Honourable Cynthia Perthwell Albert, and—she had lived.

Cynthia had been on the stage; Cynthia had been divorced; Cynthia had written a slim volume of scandalous memoirs; and eventually (the last hope of all whose meat and drink is publicity) it was announced that she was taking the veil. Unfortunately, at that time another popular figure in the social world decided to go into a convent, and Cynthia contradicted the report and announced that she had joined the Far Afield Missionary Society, and that henceforth she intended devoting her life to the heathen in his darkness.

"Yes, sir," said Bones, "I know the dear old lady. She has pots of money—bless my soul, what a silly old josser she must be to go missionary!"

He did not realise (nor, for the matter of that, did Cynthia) that in her heart had been born a great exaltation that was seven-tenths sincere—a desire for saintliness. Naturally, such a grand emotion could not be maintained at its highest level all the time, but at odd moments Cynthia, with the thought of reaching a plane of super-excellence which would endure beyond the limit of impulse, saw herself followed by adoring crowds of respectable natives; she imagined pilgrimages of native worshippers to her shrine (which she somehow managed to site in Westminster Abbey); and in her more ecstatic mood she canvassed the possibility of the Church going back to Rome, if only for long enough to procure canonisation for Saint Cynthia. In these spiritual periods Cynthia was very earnest indeed, and she was helped thereto by the character of the Founder and President of the Far Afield Mission, who was a very good old man and had the gift of making those with whom he talked feel almost as good. Cynthia, of course, had her lapses.

She came to Headquarters with eight trunks, four suit-cases and a morocco-leather dressing-bag, and she wore the beautiful white dress and helmet in which she had been photographed before she left her palatial home in Sunningdale. But the pre-martyr and saintly expression that appeared in the illustrated weeklies was conspicuously absent when Bones, gallantly wading into the sea to carry her from the surf-boat, stumbled and dropped her into the water.

"How perfectly stupid of you—you've ruined my dress," she snapped. "The man would have carried me ashore without trouble. Why the hell did you interfere?"

"Steady the buffs, dear old missionary lady," murmured

the shocked Bones. "Children present, dear old Joan of Arc!"

There were no children present except Bones, but, as he pointed out afterwards, there might have been.

"Well—why were you so careless?"

The Hon. Cynthia realised that she was not "in character" and adopted a meeker tone. She stood on the beach, shaking her soddened skirts, a picture of unsaintly annoyance. And, when she got to the Residency:

"I think, Mr. Sanders, that at least you might have had a car or something at the beach to bring me here. It was terrible walking over that awful sand, and that wretched boy, with his 'dear old lady' this and 'dear old missionary' that, is simply insufferable."

Sanders looked at her with patient interest. She was rather pretty, in a powdery, red-lipped way. Her features were good, her eyes were rather fine; she exhaled a faint and illusive fragrance.

"What are your plans, Mrs. Albert?" he asked. "I understand that you are going into the back country and that you are taking over the work of Mrs. Klein."

"I am not taking over anybody's work—I am joining her," said Cynthia.

"Then I'm afraid you'll have to go to heaven," said Sanders good-humouredly. "Mrs. Klein died three months ago. She—er—met with an accident."

Cynthia went pale.

"They didn't tell me that," she said breathlessly. "Accident——?"

"To be exact, she was murdered," said Sanders calmly, and the fragrant lady caught hold of the table.

"Murdered?"—hollowly.

Sanders nodded.

"The natives in that part are rather simple people. They loved her so much that, at the first rumour of her leaving, they killed her, as they explained, because they wanted her holy body with them."

The society missionary found a difficulty in speaking.

"They told me . . . quite safe . . ." she said at last. "Great heavens! I wouldn't dream of going to such an awful place!"

"I think you had better go home," said Sanders bluntly. "A ship calls here next Monday——"

"Certainly not!" said the Honourable Cynthia.

Go home! Be the laughing-stock of people like Julia Hawthill, who had been photographed in the beautiful habit of a novitiate and would probably still be in the Convent of Sacre Cœur (she arranged to stay at least three months), and brave the photographers and the paragraphists and the folk who would meet her at Ascot and say "Hallo, Cynthia! Thought you'd been eaten by cannibals"? It was not possible.

"There must be a nice place where I can stay and—er—do My Work? Mr. Billberry said that the mission had a station at the—what do they call it? It begins with an 'I'?"

"Isisi?" suggested Sanders. "Yes, I believe your people have a sub-station there. I'll fix it for you."

The Isisi were at this time a well-behaved people—except in the matter of the Yellow Ghosts, and that Sanders, for the moment, was not taking too seriously. He sent Bones up-river in the *Wiggle*, and the message that came back was reassuring.

The missionary was on the point of making one of his long tours in the forest, and would be away with his wife for three months. He placed his pleasant little house at Cynthia's disposal, together with lay workers and interpreters. To Cynthia he sent a long epistle full of words beginning with capitals, such as Faith, Sacrifice, Grace, and Glory. Cynthia read the letter twice to discover whether there was a bath-room in the house.

Bones took her to the Field of her Labours.

"What you've got to do, dear old miss," he said (amongst other things), "is to avoid getting your jolly old legs bitten by mosquitoes, take a tot of whisky every night at sundown, an' keep up your blessed old pecker."

"I wish you wouldn't 'dear old miss' me," said Cynthia severely. "It is very impertinent."

"Sórry, dear old missionary," murmured the prudent Bones.

Cynthia did not like her new home, though the novelty of the surroundings was delightful. She spent two days photographing the village, and had herself photographed by a native lay preacher, surrounded by little children who wore no clothes and smelt queerly.

The nights were the worst. In the daytime she could amuse herself with the camera and read the lessons in the thatched church, but the nights were awfully dark and still, and the Christian girl in the next room snored and talked in her sleep about her lover—one M'gara, the Akasava fisherman. Happily, Cynthia did not understand Bomongo and never knew that the scandals of Mayfair have a strong family likeness to the scandals of the Isisi River. For M'gara was a married man and no gentleman.

Then came a new interest in life, for, just as she was getting very bored, Cynthia made a notable convert—Osaku, son of a great witch-doctor, and himself skilled in the arts of magic and necromancy. He was a tall man. "A noble-looking savage," Cynthia described him in her first letter home. "And so awfully nice. I gave him a cake of soap—one of those we bought at Pinier's in Paris—and now he simply haunts the place. Apparently this Sanders person has treated him abominably: threatened to hang him, and did actually kill poor Osaku's father. My dear, these natives simply worship me! They call me Mama, and I feel simply uplifted. There is a most awful bathroom at this wretched little hole, but the bed is comfortable. I'm coming home on leave in three months' time. . . ."

It was true that Sanders had threatened Osaku and had ill-treated his parent—who was a famous witch-man in his day.

The position of a witch-doctor in the River Territories

is not altogether a sinecure. In the early period of Sanders's commissionership there was a sort of convention of
these Devil Men. They met in the light of a new moon on
the Island of Skulls, which is near the Pool of Black
Water, and they sent a message to Sanders asking for a
tribute to their greatness, for in these times they were very
haughty men, and chiefs and kings were in the hollow of
their hands. Sanders sent a tribute: a long rope with a
noose at the end that ran through a leather eye. And he
directed, by his messenger, that the rope should be swung
over the branch of a tree, and bade such as desired tribute
to await his coming in the first hour of that night. When
he arrived the meeting-place was deserted and the dangling
rope swayed in the night wind about the grey ashes of
their fires.

Sometimes men become witch-doctors by reason of
their hereditary right; sometimes they are just poor, mad
folk who hear strange voices; sometimes they reach their
status by cunning—Cheku, the Isisi man and father of
Osaku, was one of these. He practised secret rites in the
forest, enlisting in this manner recruits to the Leopards,
that most dangerous of all secret societies, and when the
order was stamped out he became Agent for the Yellow
Ghosts, a society which had its origin in Nigeria and
differed from the Leopards in the way of its killings.

Bosambo, chief of the Ochori, having offended these
Ghosts by his crude and brutal intrusion into one of their
séances, was marked for death. In the middle of the night,
when he slept, two men of the Isisi crept up from the river
carrying a great lump of wet clay kneaded until it was
wetly plastic. They went like shadows into his hut, and
the stronger dropped the clay over his face and fell across
him, whilst his companion lay heavily across his legs. By
all reckoning Bosambo should have been dead in two
minutes, but he had the strength of ten men. . . .

In the light of the outside fire stirred to a blaze, the
chief of the Ochori gave judgment on the yellow-faced
assassins.

"Let them go back to their land," he said, and four of his guard took the prisoners to their canoe and paddled them to a deep hole in the river. Here they tied very heavy stones to their ankles and dropped them into the water, and that night there were two new shapes on the Ghost Mountains, where the spirits of the dead dwell eternally.

Some news of this came to Sandi and he journeyed north, travelling night and day. His interview with Bosambo was brief; his stay in the village of Cheku was unpleasantly protracted.

Day after day he sat in the palaver house smelling out ghosts; night after night the three palaver fires at the foot of the tiny hillock where the house was set, burnt till near the dawn, and in the end Sanders crooked his finger at the witch-man and that was the end of him.

To Osaku, his son and successor, Sandi spoke.

"I go back to my fine house at the River End," he said, "and you stay here alive. Now this is a saying of the river, which all men know and you best of all: 'Men who stand still do not step on thorns.' Beware how you move, Osaku, lest you go the way of your father."

For the space of a year Osaku, the son of Cheku, stepped gingerly. He prophesied—but there was no harm in that. Sanders had news of wonders promised and fulfilled; of great shoals of fish indicated and found; of sons promised and born; of storms foretold that burst in due course; and only when Osaku prophesied death, and death came, did he interfere.

He sent for Osaku to come to him at the village of K'fori, where he was holding a marriage palaver, and when the tall, good-looking young man stood before him, Sanders spoke.

"O Prophet, I see you!" said he. "Let Sandi, who is your father and mother, look wisely into to-morrow. This I see, Osaku: on a certain day you shall foretell the death of your enemy, and lo! in the morning he is dead! Yet before nightfall comes Tibbetti with soldiers, and they take Osaku into the deep woods where only the monkeys live, and there they hang him by the neck, as they hanged his father. Do I prophesy well, Osaku?"

Osaku shuffled his feet and wriggled his toes, and went home hating the man with the horrible blue eyes. For the space of two moons he considered his position, and at the end of that time he borrowed half a dozen paddlers from his chief and friend and went down to Headquarters. He arrived three days before the coming of Cynthia.

"Lord," said he, "I have thought many strange thoughts. You are the father and mother of your people; you carry us in your arms and make us very happy. Now, lord, I have been gifted by devils so that my bright eyes see all that will come with the sun. And because I love you, Sandi, I will speak to all the people who listen and believe me, and tell them how beautiful you are. And I will tell them that if they are good men and pay their taxes, and do not take their spears to one another, they will be very happy, their crops shall swell, and the fish shall live in their waters."

"That will be a very good palaver," said Sanders, waiting for what would follow.

"But, lord, there will be no profit for Osaku in this," the seer went on, "since men do not give rich presents for the pleasures that are shared by all. Now this I ask, Sandi, that you shall remit all my taxes and give me presents of cloth and other wonderful things——"

"Go back to your village, Osaku," Sanders broke in unpleasantly. "I reward men, not by giving but by not taking. This is the way of governments. And because I have left you your life and your legs free from chains, I have rewarded you well. This palaver is finished."

Sanders allowed his wrathful visitor two days' grace to rest his paddlers, and in that time Osaku's brain was busy with schemes of vengeance.

Particularly was he interested in the peculiar behaviour of a very tall lieutenant of Houssas who wore a shining glass in his eye and was reputedly the son of Sandi.

Every morning after his bath, Lieutenant Tibbetts

walked down to the beach to view the progress of his
foster child. It lay in the hot sand, a large and queerly-
shaped egg. On such a morning, when he was replacing
the sand, he saw the egg crack and a tiny yellow snout
push through into the open air. Fascinated, he watched
the tiny lizard form creep out and lie palpitating violently
in the warm rays of the morning sun.

Very carefully he picked up the little creature in his
handkerchief. It squirmed feebly, but in triumph he carried his child up the Residency steps and laid it before his
superior.

"Basil has arrived—it's a boy," said Bones.

Captain Hamilton looked and shuddered.

"Take the beastly thing off the table—good Lord—
crocodiles for breakfast!"

"Dear old Ham," said Bones earnestly, "don't despise
the humble but necessary croc. He's human, dear old
Ham, the same as me; he's one of nature's artful little
tricks, Ham—the same as you. Basil will prove that with
careful an' tender nursin', even a jolly old simoonian——"

" 'Silurian' is the word you want."

"Whatever it is, can become attached to his owner.
Basil will follow me round an' sleep outside my door at
nights, Ham. That young feller—here, wake up!"

The small reptile lay very still and pale; the heavings
of his semi-transparent sides had grown imperceptible.

"Got any brandy, dear old sir?" asked Bones in
alarm.

"Drown it," said the callous Hamilton. "If you want to
revive it—sing to it. One of those old crocodile lullabies."

Bones seized the milk jug and splashed its contents into
a saucer. He thrust the sharp snout of the dying crocodile
into the white fluid. The crocodile wriggled convulsively,
opened his mouth, squawked and, whipping its head
round, suddenly gripped Bones's finger between two
rows of needle-like teeth.

"Ouch!" yelled Bones. "You low little viper—gerrout!"

He shook his hand free and the tiny beast fell on the

table, facing Bones with open mouth, its sides heaving healthily.

"By gum, dear old Ham—bit the hand that fed him! You naughty old insect! Into the river *you* go!"

When he came back from his mission of disinheritance:

"If you want to carry crocodiles around, Bones, do you mind not using the sugar-tongs?" asked Hamilton gently.

"Drew blood, dear old sir." Bones was quivering with indignation. "After what I did for him!"

"Did he drown?" asked Hamilton, his eyes glued on the month-old newspaper he was reading.

"No, sir; the dirty little dog swam like a—a frog, sir. I hope he gets into serious trouble."

Osaku had witnessed the casting off of the foster child. Squatting on the edge of the river with his paddlers, he saw the wriggling shape plop into the river, and an idea began to form in his mind. What is prophecy but inspiration? And what is inspiration but an automatic sense of cause and effect? There was one more crocodile in the river, one more slinking shape to pull down women who go to the river in the morning to draw water. A long time after Osaku had departed, disquieting news came down the river. Osaku was prophesying mightily and the Yellow Ghosts had appeared in the Akasava and the Isisi.

He foretold that there would come a great rain and the skies would spout water for three days, and at the end of that time it would cease. And then, when the new moon came, there would be a flood and the world would be covered with water, and out of the water would come a multitude of crocodiles, so many that they covered the land, and not even the little monkeys in the trees would escape them, nor the birds that flew. And all this would happen because Sandi hated the people and had filled the river with the yellow horrors that bark at night.

Sanders heard the story, stacked wood in the foredeck of the *Zaire* and kept steam, ready for an instant departure.

"All this," said Hamilton bitterly, "arises out of your infernal experiment in crocodile incubation."

Bones closed his eyes patiently.

"Be fair, dear old Ham," he pleaded. "Did I incubate the rain—I ask you, dear old Solomon? Be honest, Ham. Don't put everything on to poor old Bones. Basil was a disappointment. They happen in every family, dear old captain and adjutant."

"I shouldn't be surprised," said Sanders thoughtfully, "if that wretched little crocodile of yours was the cause of the trouble, Bones. The only thing we can do is to sit tight and hope that a miracle doesn't happen, or, if it happens, that it doesn't extend. And in the meantime, be ready to withdraw that wretched Albert woman from the Isisi."

"What miracle are you expecting, sir?" asked Hamilton in surprise.

"Crocodiles," said Sanders laconically. "It's a queer coincidence that Bosambo notified me this morning that every creek in the Ochori seems alive with them!"

Hamilton stared at him. Bones collapsed into a chair.

"Not Basil?" he said weakly. "Little Basil hasn't had time to raise a family. . . ."

"It happened before, about twelve years ago, according to reports. The Colonial Office zoologist has a theory that there is a species of croc who buries himself in the mud and only makes an appearance once in a blue moon—I've dug out these fellows myself, buried twelve feet under the river bed and very annoyed to be awakened from their sleep."

That very night the phenomenon he dreaded was demonstrated at the very doors of the Residency. It was two o'clock in the morning and the moon showed fitfully, when Abdulla, the sentry before the guard's hut, saw something moving stealthily across the parade-ground and challenged. At the sound of his voice the creature remained still for a long time, and the sentry decided that it was a moon shadow he had seen, until he saw it move again, this time towards him and there came to his sensitive nostrils a faint scent of musk. His Lee-Metford went up immediately.

Sanders heard the sound of the shot, and came out on to the stoep, revolver in hand. He heard Bones's high-pitched voice speaking from the door of his hut, but Sanders was too far away to hear the conversation.

"What is it, sir?" Hamilton was at the Commissioner's side, his rifle under his arm.

"I thought I heard a shot fired. Something's wrong—do you hear Bones?"

They heard Bones at that moment; a raucous squawk of fear, then, from the direction of his hut, came the staccato rattle of his automatic.

"Good God! Look!" gasped Sanders.

A gap in the clouds sent a sudden flood of moonlight over the parade-ground. Three—four—five, he counted; great lizard shapes that ran swiftly towards the river. Hamilton fired, and one of the things jerked convulsively, uttered a bellowing roar of pain, crawled a little farther and lay still. As it did so, the largest of the fugitives lashed round and, without warning, came straight for the Residency steps at an incredible pace. Hamilton and the Commissioner fired together; fired again, apparently without effect. It was not till the long head was thrusting up towards the stoep that the third shot took effect.

"Jumping Moses!" breathed Hamilton.

By this time lights were showing in all the huts. The guard were firing at something they could not see, and, jamming another cartridge into the chamber of his rifle, Hamilton sprinted across the parade-ground towards Bones's hut.

He found his junior sprawled on the ground, and at first he thought he was dead, and then that his leg was broken. Two Houssas hauled Bones into the Residency, and laid him flat on the floor.

"The devil must have caught him with its tail," said Hamilton, as he forced brandy between the clenched teeth.

Bones opened his eyes.

"Not Basil," he murmured. "Poor little Basil . . .!"

"Wake up, you poultry farmer!" snarled Hamilton, and Bones sat upright, rubbed his leg, and stared around.

"It was not Basil," he said solemnly. "I'd like to make a statement before I die, dear old sir, exonerating poor little Basil. . . ."

It was a quarter of an hour before his scattered senses were put in order, and he had little to tell that was informative. He had heard the shot, rushed out of his hut, and had seen two horrible eyes glittering at him, and had fired. And that was all that he remembered.

When daylight came there arrived three canoes from villages in the neighbourhood, with stories of disaster and murder. Huts had been broken and entered; women and children and old men had disappeared; but the greatest casualties had occurred in the little compound where the village kept its edible dogs. The Residency area, fortunately, had suffered no loss.

"If this sort of thing occurs here," said Sanders, worried, "what is happening on the Upper River?"

He was standing on the deck of the *Zaire* looking out over the black and swollen sea. The river was alive with crocodiles; their ripples showed at every turn. Sanders gathered the families into the thick woods that lay at the extreme centre of the little peninsula on which the Residency stood.

"Have fires lit on the parade-ground to-night," he gave orders. "Hamilton, you had better remain here in charge. I'll take Bones to the Upper River."

At eleven o'clock that morning the *Zaire* set out on its trip. The river was deserted; no human craft was in sight, which was not remarkable, since the waters were running at between eight and nine knots; and his progress was a slow one. He steamed all night, stopping only to replenish his fuel at the village of Igebi. Here he began to realise the full extent of the disaster. The village was a ruin; scarcely a hut stood squarely on its foundations. The night before, a trembling headman told him, "all the crocodiles in the world" had come up out of the water, and what damage they had done he was not able to say because his people, except his own son, had fled to the woods. The casualties had been heavy. He told stories which would have sickened the average man, and Sanders listened with seeming impassivity, loaded up his wood and continued his journey.

All the way up, six Houssa marksmen had sat in the bow, shooting at every crocodile they saw. Once, rounding a bend of the river, they came upon a long, narrow bank of sand, covered with the reptiles. Bones got the Hotchkiss gun into action and sent two shrapnel shells bursting over the wriggling mass. In a second the sand strip was clear, save for two lame shapes.

He tied up at the village of the Lesser Isisi and found it deserted. There was ghastly evidence in the streets of the overnight raid.

Sanders thought of the missionary, and went white.

"Lord, that Mama has gone," said the man. "I went by the forest path to her hut and I saw nothing but a dead woman who had been speared——"

"Speared?" snarled Sanders.

"Somebody killed her," said the trembling man. "Who knows what devils walk on such a night?"

The missionary hut was a mile from the town, and when Sanders got there he found nothing but a dead girl at the door of Cynthia's room. A devil had walked that night more potent than the lizards that came out of the water.

· · · · · ·

When the rains continued to fall, Osaku had grown frightened, and called together his four disciples.

"Now this is the end of the world," he said; "for Sandi will know that I have brought this rain, and if the Terrible Ones follow, then Sandi will come and there will be an end to me, and to all of us who have made this thing by our magic. And if we hang for such a little thing, what shall happen if we do other deeds? For no man has more than one life, and if he kills one or kills all the world, no worse can come to him."

In this long-winded way did he paraphrase the saying that they might as well be hung for a sheep as a lamb.

"Let us take the Jesu-mama to a certain island in the lake where Sandi never goes, and will not be wise to look. For this woman loves me and has given me wonderful things, but because she fears Sandi she turns her face from me. And you shall bring whoever has gladdened your bed, and we will live happily and teach one another magic."

His followers, themselves alarmed by the downpour, went their way.

Cynthia was lying down in her hut, listening to the ceaseless drumming of the rain, and wondering how long it would be before Sanders could send a launch for her, when she heard voices in the outer room and the sound of a squeal. She rose hastily as the grass door was pushed aside. Osaku said something in a language she did not understand, but his beckoning hand spoke all tongues.

As she came trembling into the dark outer room, she trod on something that yielded to her foot, and she screamed—there was blood on Osaku's spear, for the girl who snored, as she dreamt of her fisherman lover, snored no more.

They passed into the teeming rain, Osaku's hand on her arm, and she was thrust into a narrow canoe that wobbled horribly. The reeking paddler sent the craft along the bank and, turning abruptly, drove straight into the narrow creek which leads to the lake. Dawn brought them to the wide waters and to a small island. It was not the destination that Osaku had intended, but the canoe was half full of rain water, and though two men baled continuously they could not keep pace with the downpour.

"Here we stay, Mama," said Osaku, and dragged the half-dead girl to land. She was stiff and numb, frozen with terror.

Under the dripping trees, they plaited her a rough covering of grass, and under this she dozed and swooned throughout the last day of the rains. The lake had risen, and there were certain disturbances which troubled Osaku and his companions, for the rain-pitted surface of the waters was laced with significant ripples, and once he saw two shining crocodiles waddle out of the lake and lie down on the shore. Now a crocodile, when he takes to land, keeps his snout pointed to the water, ready to dive at the least alarm—but these great reptiles pointed their wicked noses to the land. Osaku had a thought.

"It seems," he said, "that the Mama has a greater magic than we. I have heard of such things from the God-men, and now I know that it is true; the yellow ones are their ju-ju—did not Tibbetti hold one in his hand? If we do this Mama no harm they will go away. Presently we will go to to the big island where they cannot reach us, and then we will do what we wish."

There were ten people on his islet, which was growing smaller as the waters rose. Each of the four had brought his companion—and only one of these had come willingly. Through the haze of her sick dreams Cynthia heard the wails and lamentations of the rest and shivered.

In the night she was awakened by a horrible sound and flew out into the open. The dawn was near at hand, and the crescent of the morning moon hung low.

Screams and gruff, throaty barkings; the flogging of grass and bush by terrible tails.

. . . . .

Sanders picked up the trail from a half-crazed fisherman, and the *Zaire* came to the island with the first rays of the sun. Bones, gun in hand, leapt ashore. There was no evidence of horror—nothing but trodden bushes and the broken saplings, with a trace of blood here and there.

Cynthia was standing alone, her frail figure rigid, a quiet smile on her face.

". . . they did not touch me because I am a saint . . . you realise that, of course, Mr. Tibbetts? It was rather horrid seeing them pulled into the water, but the wretched things simply did not touch me at all! I wish you would send a paragraph to the *Morning Post*—Saint Cynthia!"

She smiled weakly into his face, her lips trembling, her eyes set in a dreadful stare.

"The natives adore me—don't forget that, please. And would you tell my chauffeur that I'm quite ready to go home?"

And then she fell into his arms, and he carried her to the *Zaire*.

Quite a lot of people think that the Honourable Cynthia is still in the Dark Land, and in a sense they are right. But it is in the dark land of what is euphemistically called a Nursing Home in the north of London, where Cynthia sits with her quiet smile and her staring eyes and talks familiarly of saints and crocodiles.

VI

THE MAN WHO HATED SHEFFIELD

BEYOND the Forest of Happy Dreams, which is a pestilential marsh, beautiful to see but deadly to traverse, lie the hunting grounds of the Isisi people; and beyond that again, the outliers of the N'gombi, a tribe which is sometimes called the Lesser N'gombi and sometimes the N'gombi Isisi, which means very much the same thing.

Here, in the depths of the primeval forest, unexploited by any save the hunters and the folk who collect rubber, lived, out of contact with their neighbours, and terribly jealous of interference, a certain sub-tribe who were called the Bald Men of I'fubi. They made no wars, stole neither goats nor women, lived without salt, and existed without any offence to any.

Once a year came Sanders, toiling through the forest, on his annual visit to these wayward children of his; but when he sat in palaver, to hear the accumulated grievances of the year, there was nothing to be told except that some luckless man of the Isisi or the Greater N'gombi had trespassed on their reserves or had killed their monkeys. Of private quarrels he never heard; he asked few questions and suspected much.

A rumour had reached him of a man of the tribe who had beaten his wife with great cruelty, and had defied his chief; but when Sanders came after, and expected to hear charges against the rebel, none was laid. And when, most discreetly, he asked what had happened to the man, they told him airily that he had died of the sickness *mongo*, and pointed out his shallow grave, where the torn shreds of his linen fluttered feebly and the broken cooking-pots of his house were scattered around. Also they showed him the place where his hut had been, and now all that Sanders could see was a drunken roof, half hidden by the elephant grass, and very wisely he did not pursue his inquiry any further. The "sickness *mongo*" might mean anything from beri-beri to the bright, curved executioner's knife which hung everlastingly at the entrance of the old chief's hut.

These Bald Men—and it is a curious fact that the heads even of the youth of the tribe shone like polished ebony—gave no trouble; carried no spears to the killing of their neighbours; paid their taxes regularly; were clean and industrious; and if they practised secret rites and concocted strange medicants, such as had never been heard of by any other people of the river, there was no blood-letting, so far as was known, and they served a most useful purpose, in that they stood, in their jealousy, as guardians of the Pans which stretched behind the forest, an unnatural plain, innocent of bush or tree for forty square miles. It was a legend amongst all the Europeans of the coast that the Pans were rich in alluvial gold. Certainly Government never sought to test the truth of this, putting in the balance, against such a discovery, the certainty of an influx of most undesirable people, who follow every discovery of gold.

There came into this quiet land a white man, who called himself Odwall. It had once been Obenwitsch, but, for reasons of his own, he had anglicised himself, taken off the beard he had been in the habit of wearing, and thus, outwardly changed, strayed into the region of the Pans, which are approachable only through the country of the Bald Men. These quiet souls, who believed that there were only three white men in the world, received Mr. Odwall with the profound respect and dazed wonder which a church convention might offer to a second, and hitherto unsuspected, Archbishop of Canterbury.

He sat down and talked to them in their own language, and they gave a great feast and a dance of girls, and they told him of their mystery, and why their heads were bald; but in this he was not greatly interested. Nor was he especially thrilled when old Ch'uga, chief of the village, told him secretly, in a whisper and in the darkest corner of his hut, that a new herb had been found which cured madness. For the Bald Men are very wise in the use of herbs, and because of this they are bald, as you shall learn.

Tactfully and gradually, he led the talk round to the subject of the Pans and the yellow dust that could be washed from the dark earth; but Ch'uga shook his head at the first word of it.

"Lord," said he, a trifle shocked, "these things we do not talk about, because of Sandi our father, nor do we dig into the earth, for that also is forbidden. And when strange men come and make little holes in the ground, we fight them with our spears and they run away."

Mr. Obenwitsch (we had better call him Odwall) was terribly interested but asked no further questions. He had, he calculated, at least three months to get better acquainted with the chief, and he could afford to bide his time.

It was unfortunate for him that, the following morning, as he strolled through the tree-fringed village street, he met another white man, who walked out of the forest, followed by six red-tarboshed soldiers. Mr. Odwall did not swoon; he made a little grimace which might have been mistaken for a smile, and touched the rim of his none-too-clean helmet.

"Good morning, Mr. Commissioner," he said. "My name's Odwall——"

"Your name is Obenwitsch," said Sanders, with his hard little smile. "Three years ago I had the satisfaction of kicking you out of this country, and I have an idea that I'm going to repeat that process, but this time, I think, the kick will be harder."

Mr. Odwall was nearly a head taller than the dapper Commissioner; he was heavily built and something of a rough fighter; but he took the threat meekly, and it was not only the presence of the soldiers that restrained him.

"You're in reserved territory without a permit," said

Sanders, "and that may not be all. I'd like to see your baggage."

The baggage, which consisted of a weather-worn grip, was brought from the chief's hut (all the Bald Men standing round, clasping their sides anxiously and wondering what was toward). Sanders opened the grip and turned over its contents. There was a quart flask of rye whisky, and this he smelt, afterwards turning the contents upon the ground.

"You're carrying spirits in a prohibited area," he said briefly, "and I shall commit you to prison with hard labour for six months."

"See here, Sanders, you're acting a little arbitrarily——"

"You can go quietly or you can go in irons," interrupted Sanders. "I won't argue with you."

Mr. Obenwitsch went down the river, a prisoner under escort, to Headquarters, and forthwith was committed to prison.

Sanders did not explain to the Bald Men why he had taken his fellow-countryman away, for it was his business to keep up the end of the European race, and Mr. Odwall knew him well enough to be certain of his reticence. He served his six months and was deported to England, for he was a British subject. But there was in his heart no malice towards Sanders, for Walter Odwall was an habitual breaker of the law, and such men respect authority.

He came to London with enough money to hire a flat in Jermyn Street and to arrange with a high-class stationer for certain printing. For six months he had sat in prison, planning and re-planning, and his scheme was complete in all respects save one, and this deficiency could easily be remedied. He called to him a financier.

He had met Mr. Wilberry in one of those social capillaries which are erroneously described as night clubs. Capillaries indeed, for here the poison gas of spurious Bohemianism intermingles with the good red blood of commerce, with disastrous effects. Mr. Wilberry was a

well-to-do manufacturer whose chief characteristic was
that he hated Sheffield. His hatred was such an obsession
with him that he would have gone a hundred miles out of
his way to avoid the town. When he wrote to the manager
of his factory (which was indubitably in Sheffield) he had
the envelope addressed by his secretary—the word was so
hateful that he could not write it.

He was not only a manufacturer, but an experimental
chemist, having taken a very high science degree, and his
hobby and preoccupation was a new kind of steel which
was to revolutionise the trade. If the truth be told, he was
a better business man than a scientist, and when, at the cost
of a hundred thousand pounds, he produced in triumph a
steel which was at once stainless and malleable, and offered
Sheffield the privilege (in exchange for a small royalty
which a disinterested statistician calculated would bring
him in about three millions a year) of manufacturing this
super-article, Sheffield was at first interested, then sceptical; applied tests, with unfortunate results, and the end
of it was that the Sheffield manufacturers in council
assembled, and aided and supported by their technical
experts, spoke slightingly of Wilberry Steel, refused either
to purchase or to manufacture it, and there the matter
finished, in so far as they were concerned.

Mr. Wilberry never forgave Sheffield; he loathed
Sheffield with a loathing beyond the understanding of any
who have not seen the child of their dreams massacred by
cruel and ruthless hands. He sold his estate in the neighbourhood of the hated town; would have closed down his
extensive works, only he was a business man, and that
would have been an unbusinesslike thing to do; and
settled in Surrey with a large laboratory, where he employed any scientific young gentleman who held the same
view about Wilberry Steel as he held.

Odwall had marked this gentleman for exploitation.
He knew little or nothing about steel, but whilst he was in
prison he had had the advantage of reading Volume XIV
of the jail's encyclopædia, and a careful study of the

article on iron told him that no story he might tell of an ore-field in the Territories would arouse the least enthusiasm in the bosom of Mr. Wilberry. For iron must be found near coal, and there must be easy transportation.

In his stuffy little sitting-room overlooking Jermyn Street he expanded his scheme.

"Gold interests everybody," he said; "it interests you, Mr. Wilberry; it interests the boy in the street. . . ."

He proceeded to tell the story of the Pans and his audience was impressed.

Mr. Wilberry was a moist, red-faced man who smoked large cigars and wore white spats and a diamond ring. Smallish eyes and a little black moustache complete the description. He was very rich and very sceptical, until Mr. Odwall showed him a little bag filled with dull yellow grains.

"I managed to wash out a bucketful of dirt, and that is what I got," he said impressively.

The interested financier did not ask how it came about that Mr. Odwall had succeeded in smuggling his find through the rigorous searchings which are part of prison discipline. If he had asked, he would have been told an elaborate lie, for the gold was bought from a man in Dakka on the homeward voyage.

"I don't mind putting a couple of thousand into it," said Mr. Wilberry. "Those thick-headed swine of Sheffield have almost ruined me, and some day, my boy, I'm going to get back on 'em! I'd give half a million to twist the blighters!"

His statement did not accord with his protestations of poverty, but Odwall was not the type of man who boggled at an inconsistency.

His plan was a simple one.

"There's a kid officer out there," he said, "who would fall for anything with a tale to it. In June, Sanders goes up to the Ochori for his palavers with the northern chiefs, and he'll take Captain Hamilton with him." He explained Hamilton's position and identity. "This time I'll have three months' clear run of the Territory, and if I get on the right side of this kid Tibbetts I'll have the claims staked and registered before Sanders is back."

"Does Tibbetts know you?"

"Not from a crow. He was away when Sanders brought me down-river, and he wasn't in the Territory when I was trading there. Leave it to me!"

    .   .   .   .

Bones was surprised at nothing except the inability of his superior officer to appreciate his undoubted musical gifts. But the letter from "Mr. Walter Bagen" was so unexpected and so unusual of character that Lieutenant Tibbetts of the King's Houssas spent a whole hour blessing his own soul. Nevertheless, he lost no time in replying.

> "*Dear Sir,*" he wrote, "*I have the honnour to acknowledge the receit of your leter your letter. Of the 15th ultimus. I thank you also for refereing reffering to me as (a great authiroty authroity authoritey)*"—Bones had never solved the mystery of the inverted comma—"*on the subject of archæology.*" (He got this one right because he copied it letter by letter from his correspondent's typewritten epistle.) "*I will certainley take a note of anything annything unusual in the way of Roman remains Roman remains evedence of early civvilisation et cet et cet. I thank you for illecting me a Fellow of the Central African Arkilogicle Society*" (this time he wrote the word from memory) "*and anything I can do to help foreward the great course of Arch of the Society you can depend on me doing. Trusting you are well,*
>   *Sincerely,*
>   A. Tibbetts, Lt., F.C.A.A.S.

At tiffin, Bones mentioned his new honour very casually.

"Fellow of the what?" asked Hamilton, his dark face screwed up inquiringly.

"Archi—um—you know, dear old officer . . . fossils an'

things." Bones coughed and looked serious and important. "I shouldn't be a bit surprised if I didn't find something—a dina—um—one of those jolly old birds that used to fly around in prehistoric days, Ham, when you were a child, so to speak. And the dinky little ich—something—you find *his* bones almost anywhere. An' Roman remains——"

"Are you going to write a lot of slush about these things?" asked Captain Hamilton coarsely.

Bones raised his eyebrows and looked hurt.

"I only ask," said Hamilton, "because I've had a sarcastic letter from the Accountant-General, who wants to know how many 'l's' there are in 'flannel'—I gather that he has been studying your store report."

Lieutenant Tibbetts fixed his monocle more firmly in his eye.

"I usually use three, but there may be four, Ham," he said, with gentle reproach. "The point is, flannel shirts have nothin' to do with archy—you know the word."

The essay on "Roman Fosils and Other Articals of Ancient Origoin" has never seen the light, because Mr. Bagen, whose other name was Odwall, was not really interested in archæology, no matter how it was spelt, and the Society had no existence, except on the notepaper he had printed for the purpose of conferring the Fellowship upon Bones. The letter which came back, and which was headed in heavily embossed type:

"The Institute of the Central Africa
Archæological Society,
943, Jermyn Street.
President: The Duke of ——
Secretary: Walter S. Bagen, F.C.A.A.S.

acknowledged Bones's essay, "which will be printed in the Proceedings of the Society," and informed him:

"*It is the intention of the Society to send a small party of scientists to the Coast in the near future, and an effort will be made, either by His Grace the President, or by the writer, to call and offer you the Society's congratulations upon your admirable contribution to our knowledge of an obscure and fascinating subject."*

It was on a hot day in June that the representative of the Central African Archæological Society walked slowly up the beach, where he had been landed from a surf-boat, a prayer on his lips that nothing had happened to interfere with Mr. Sanders's departure. Mr. Odwall wore white duck, a white helmet, his shoes were white—he was in his person an illustration of scientific purity. His heavy horn-rimmed glasses, no less than the volume he carried under his arm, gave him a grave and studious appearance.

"Sandi he no lib, sah," said the Houssa sergeant who met him half-way, and Mr. Odwall's mind was relieved of a heavy burden. "Militini he no lib, sah: he go long time up-river. Mistah Tibbetti you see um, sah?"

Odwall spoke Coast Arabic very well; he preferred for the moment to be a stranger to the land and to its many vernaculars.

Bones was lying on a long chair on the stoep, his large feet elevated to the rails. He scrambled up at the sight of the visitor.

"Bless my soul, dear old secretary!" he gasped, when the honour which was being done to him was revealed. "Never had the slightest idea you were coming——"

He was a little incoherent. Mr. Odwall gathered that, if news of his coming had been sent ahead, there would have been a band to meet him.

Over tiffin Bones grew archæological.

"There are jolly old places in this country nobody has ever explored," he said. "Roman remains! There's a sort of viaduct up in the I'fubi—you know, sir, a sort of bridge that water runs over—horribly Roman! And there's no end of"—Bones manipulated his hands convulsively—"a kind of . . . I don't know what the jolly old arch . . . what the word is for it . . . it's a sort of well

arrangement—an' yet it isn't a well, if you understand,
dear old sir . . . it's a sort of wall . . . not exactly a
wall——"

"I quite understand," said Mr. Odwall gravely; "it's
what we call an odalisque."

"That's it!" said Bones. "You've got the word I've
been tryin' to think of."

That evening Mr. Odwall put forward a tentative plan.

"Ye—es," said Bones, but with no great heartiness.
"You could go up, of course—I'd have to ask the Commissioner."

"I have a permit from the Colonial Office," suggested
Mr. Odwall.

He possessed nothing of the sort, but he had rightly
surmised that in the circumstances he would not be asked
to show any such document.

Bones was relieved.

"If you have that, dear old Archi—um—why, of course,
you can go. I'd love to come with you, but I'm sort of
stuck here till Mr. Sanders returns."

Odwall hired paddlers the next morning, loaded his kit
in the centre of the canoe and, himself comfortably en-
sconced under a palm-leaf roof, he left on his journey. In
seven days he landed at the nearest point to the Pans and
made his way through the forest. On the twelfth day he
reached the village of the Bald Men and was effusively
welcomed.

For the greater part of a week he sat down in the village, spending most of his days wandering in the desolation of the Pans—but everywhere he went the old chief
accompanied him.

"Lord, this is a bad place to go," said the old man; "for
there are ghosts and terrible ju-jus hiding in the ground.
Also it is the word of Sandi our lord, that no white man
shall walk here because of the evil which will follow.
Come with me into the green woods and I will show you a
little flower that gives men great courage if it is picked by
the light of the moon and boiled in a big pot. . . ."

Mr. Odwall had no need for such a stimulant. The dope he wanted lay in the black earth.

One night, when his stay had lasted nearly a fortnight and he had, by the exercise of his ingenuity, secured and washed a bucket of earth, without, however, discovering the slightest trace of gold, the old chief paid a visit to the hut, at the door of which Mr. Odwall sat, moodily surveying the domestic life of the village.

"Master," he said in his secretive way, "because you are a friend of Sandi I will give you a great treasure."

He looked around to see if he could be overheard, and Mr. Odwall's heart leapt.

"This is our mystery which you know. It was whispered to me by my father, the great chief K'suro, and I also will tell it to my son when the hand of death is on my face."

From under his chief's robe of dingy skins, he brought a little clay pot which was filled to the brim with a greenish-yellow substance of the consistency of butter. Mr. Odwall's jaw dropped. For one wild moment of exhilaration he had expected the withered hand to come out of the robe holding a small bag of gold.

"This is our wonder," said the chief in a hushed voice. "Because of this we are different from all other men."

He caught hold of his guest's unwilling hand, smeared a little of the green butter on his hairy arm, and then, with the edge of his robe, wiped it clean. Where there had been hair was a smooth surface.

"We are bald because of this magic," said the old chief, blissfully unconscious of the other's rising annoyance. "This I give to you because it is more wonderful than anything in the world."

Mr. Odwall's first impulse was to throw the pot at the old man's head, but he conquered this desire, and put the little jar on the ground beside him.

"That is fine talk and good magic, chief," he said briskly; "but I have heard of other wonders in this forest, such as the yellow dust that comes out of the earth. Now

I tell you that in my own country I am a very great chief and have many slaves and great riches, and I sleep upon a fine skin bed every night. And if you tell me truly where this yellow dust lies, I will make you a rich man. Your goats shall fill the forest, and the houses of your wives shall be a village.''

Ch'uga, the chief, was obviously ill at ease.

"Lord, I know of no yellow dust," he said uneasily; "nor must I speak of such, for that is Sandi's order. Once a man came to the third hole and took away dust, and that was a bad palaver, for Sandi followed him to the end of the world and caught him. Let me tell you of this strange mud of yours, and of our cunning in making it. First we take the fat of goats, and this we boil in a big pot, with the red berries——"

Mr. Odwall yawned.

"Tell me to-morrow, chief."

He had learnt all he wanted to know. The third hole —that was the third shallow pan, four miles away. That night, when the village slept, he crept forth from his hut, carrying a canvas bag which contained a big trowel, and, moving cautiously, so that the watchman might not see him, he went through a fringe of woodland and came to the desolation. Working his way round, by a circuitous route, he reached "the third hole." The ground was soft and friable, yielding to his trowel without calling for any exceptional effort of strength.

He got through the top layer and struck what he guessed was the alluvial patch, and, opening the mouth of his bag, he half filled it. He tested its weight: he could carry that back to the village and could wash the dirt at his leisure. He had risen to his feet and was twisting the neck of the bag, preparatory to hoisting it on his back, when he looked round and saw a figure standing in the moonlight. It was the old chief.

"O, ko!" said Ch'uga dismally. "This is a bad palaver, and I will send to Sandi this sad news. Master, you will empty your sack."

"Empty nothing!" snarled Odwall. And then, in Bomongo, he tried to excuse his presence. But as he sought to pass the custodian of the Pans, the old man gripped him by the arm, very gently but very strongly.

"Master, you do not go hence," he said.

Odwall tried to wrench himself free, and, finding this difficult, encumbered as he was, dropped his bag and pushed the old man back. He saw the glint of a killing spear raised in warning, and struck savagely with his sharp-edged trowel. The blow got home and the old man, stumbling to his knees, fell an inert heap. Odwall cursed his folly, and, going down on to his knees, turned the chief on to his back. He was bleeding freely, and at the sight of the still face the adventurer felt a cold chill run down his spine. Sanders would be merciless if he caught him now. There would be a rope and a tree, and his would be a name blotted out and forgotten.

He took out a handkerchief and bandaged the wound as well as he could; and then, with his sack over his shoulder and wet with perspiration, he went back to the village and, packing his grip, struck the path which led to the coast. For three days he toiled on without carriers or bearers, in the blazing heat of the tropical sun, fearful every moment of hearing the patter of footsteps behind him, sleeping on his feet as he staggered under the heavy burden of his treasure.

At last he came to where he had left his paddlers and, without more ado, he heaved bag and suit-case to the bottom of the canoe, before he dropped like a log into his place in the stern; before the paddlers began their chant, he was asleep. When he awoke it was early morning, and the canoe was tied up to the side of a little wood. He saw the red glow of the fire and put out his hand for the bag of earth which had cost him so dear. It was not there!

His hoarse yell of anger brought the headman of the paddlers to him.

"Lord, it was only earth, and was weighing down the

canoe, for the waters are rough near the Isisi River, so we threw it overboard."

Odwall raged up and down the bank like a lunatic, cursing the men, cursing Sanders, cursing everything except his own insensate folly.

Bones went down to meet the canoe as soon as it was sighted, and was shocked at the ghastly appearance of the man.

"Dear old astrologer!" he said in alarm. "You've got fever, dear old secretary. You must let me give you a little quinine——"

"When does the next boat call?"

"It's calling, dear old archi—whatever the word is. Did you find the Roman remains? That thing"—Bones's hands worked rapidly.

"Yes, yes, I found it," said the other impatiently.

He was relieved to discover that news had not already come to Headquarters of his crime. Perhaps Ch'uga was not dead. These old natives were as tough as wire.

"Won't you wait and see the Commissioner? He's returning to-morrow."

"To-morrow?" Odwall nearly screamed the word. "No, no, I must go to-day. You say the ship is calling?"

Bones pointed dramatically to the sea. A big German steamer had dropped anchor, and the surf-boat was being lowered.

The departure of Mr. Walter Bagen, Secretary of the Central African Archæological Society, was something in the nature of a disappointment to Bones, who had prepared quite a lot of interesting but inaccurate information upon a hypothetical Greek occupation of the country, based largely on the presence of a Corinthian pillar which supported the veranda of the Residency and which, if the truth be told, had been brought to the country by Sanders's predecessor.

Not until the flat shores of the River Territories had sunk beneath the rim of the ocean did Mr. Odwall feel comfortable.

The boat did not touch at another British port until it called at Plymouth. And now he could settle down to the invention of a story which would satisfy his financial supporter.

Mr. Wilberry came to the reoccupied Jermyn Street flat, well aware that he had to listen to a story of failure; for he was a business man, and was quite capable of interpreting a letter which began: "I have got back, as you will see, and although the results of my visit were not all I could have desired——"

"I am going to tell you the truth," said Odwall, when the red-faced man had settled himself comfortably in the only armchair large enough to seat him.

Oddly enough, the story the returned wanderer told was substantially true—it was the easiest and the most plausible explanation of his abortive effort.

"Bad luck," said Mr. Wilberry, who had lost money before. "But I should have thought that if you'd given the old bird enough money, he'd have helped you?"

Odwall shook his head.

"You don't know the influence that swine Sanders has over the natives," he said. And then he remembered. "Here's something that will interest you."

He went into his bedroom, brought back a small jar of native make, and, taking off the oil paper with which he had covered its contents, he showed the greenish-yellow ointment.

Mr. Wilberry frowned.

"A depilatory?" he said. "Does it work?"

"Does it work?" Odwall laughed. "It's half empty now. I've used it all the way back from Africa to save shaving."

Wilberry reached out his hand, took the pot, smeared a little on the hair by the side of his ear and, taking out his handkerchief, wiped it. A bare patch showed where the ointment had touched.

He caught his breath.

"Do you know . . . the formula for this?" he gasped.
Odwall shook his head.

"No; I didn't bother—you can get it analysed——"

"Analysed! It's a vegetable product, you fool! Analysts can't tell us anything. Did he offer you the formula?"

"Yes; I couldn't be bothered. I was after gold——"

Wilberry waved his podgy hands in despair.

"My God!" he howled, and turned around on the adventurer with blazing eyes. "You fool! You great brainless fool!" he shouted. "Gold, did you want? And you had it!" He held up the pot. "Do you realise what you've got here—what we could have had? If I had this formula I could ruin Sheffield! There wouldn't be a razor sold. . . . Oh, you short-sighted lunatic!"

"But—but——" stammered the other.

"But, but!" mimicked his patron savagely. "That pot was worth a million pounds—it was worth ten million— I'd have had half Sheffield at my feet begging for mercy; for the formula of this would have put out of business every razor, every safety razor company in the world! Gold? This is gold! Under your ugly nose and you couldn't see it!"

.   .   .   .   .

It is a strange fact that neither Bones nor Sanders associated the untimely death of the old chief with the visit of the secretary of a great archæological society. Sanders went in search of the white man, and learnt only, from the descriptions that were given, that Mr. Odwall had in some way returned to the country and had made his escape again.

"I don't know whether it's a sign of mourning or whether it's due to some other cause—the bald people are no longer bald," said Sanders at dinner on the night of his return. "Apparently they used some sort of stuff that the old chief made, and the secret of which he did not pass on to his people. Now the poor old boy's gone, the Bald

Men are becoming quite normal again. You ought to write to your archæological society about it, Bones."

A piece of advice which Bones followed, but the letter came back marked "Gone away—addressee not known."

VII

THE JOY SEEKERS

THE *Zaire* had once paid a visit to the Islands of Joy. There was a group of six, none larger than a mile in circumference, and two of them half that size; and they were uninhabited. For, although water was to be had here and vegetation grew in great abundance, there was neither monkey nor rat nor even snake.

Once upon a time the Portuguese had established a post on the island, and the grey ruins of a little fort were still visible; and there was evidence of cultivated fields. But nobody coveted the Islands of Joy; they were not even in a geographical position which would have justified the establishment of a cable station.

Bones had threatened to spend a fortnight in a botanical classification—it was at a time when he was badly bitten with the botanical fever, and kept volumes of pressed grasses and flowers, inaccurately named. But his promise was never kept, and the Islands of Joy stood for a landmark and a menace to shipping; though, if the truth be told, no regular line came within twenty miles of these pleasant rocks.

There were legends about them, and these existed far up the river, amongst people whose eyes had never rested on the sea. It was the summer home of M'shimba-M'shamba, according to one account; and populated by a race of slaves who made cloth for the white people, according to another.

The Kano people had a legend that Mahomet had once landed on the largest, and had been inspired by a dream that all the world would be converted to his teachings. But then, the Kano people invest the most commonplace spot with holy mystery.

The Houssas are Mohammedan in all their habits and practices except that they do not keep their women veiled, though Abiboo once told Mr. Commissioner Sanders that certain of the Fula—who, under the Emir, are the lords of Kano—have this custom. But if they do not segregate their womenfolk, they hold rigid views on their integrity. And when Benabdul, a soldier of the King's Houssas, coming through the wood, found his young and lovely wife struggling in the arms of Achmet the bugler, and heard her fearful screams, he flew at the good-looking youth, who had offended beyond pardon, and there would have been murder, only the sound of the affray brought Sergeant Abiboo on the scene, and Abiboo's favourite peacemaker was a stiff strip of rhinoceros hide, which hurt.

Lieutenant Tibbetts held his morning palaver at seven o'clock, and before him was marched the erring bugler and the story of his abominable deeds was told. The woman did not testify—her husband was there to speak for her. He was very voluble. When the evidence was ended, Bones fixed his monocle and gave judgment.

"You will be kept in the dark prison for seven days. All the marks on your arm that say 'this is a good soldier' shall be taken from your arm, and you shall lose your pay all the time you are in prison."

So Achmet went to the cells behind the guard-room and picked oakum on a sparse dietary.

"Better send the young fool back to H.Q.," suggested Sanders, and Captain Hamilton agreed.

But the moving of units from one station to another is not an easy matter. There were reports (in triplicate) to be made to H.Q., memoranda to answer, and this takes time. The unpopular Achmet came out of prison and resumed his bugle practice, and it looked as though matters would settle down, for Benabdul, the injured husband, was a mild man and incapable of sustaining a feud.

Not so his wife, it seemed. Her name was Fahmeh, and

she was of the Arab type, brown, and, by European standards, pretty, for her nose was thin and straight, and she had fine eyes.

It was she who kept clean the hut of Lieutenant Tibbetts and laundered his linen.

"Lord," she said one morning whilst she was at her work, "this man Achmet still looks at me as I pass him, and his eyes are terribly loving. I am afraid."

Bones had a face almost entirely covered with lather at that moment, and his bright razor was poised.

"Woman, if you did not look at him, you would not be offended," he said; "for it is written in the Sura of the Djin that offence comes from knowing."

She frowned at this.

"All the women point at me," she said, "and some ask why my husband does not beat him. Until this man goes I will not be happy, for I hate him."

"All things happen," said the philosophical young officer, and went on with his toilet.

Bones was undoubtedly working very hard just then, and had his own worries. His many musical possessions gathered dust in odd places, his portable harmonium was never opened, the bagpipes presented by a misguided administrator hung neglected (Fahmeh never even dusted them, believing them to be the dried remains of a sea monster of the octopus family).

He was working more industriously and continuously than usual at a law course. From Headquarters had come an elaborate circular urging the necessity for "all officers holding administrative positions or assistants to officers holding administrative positions, or officers who may at any time be called upon, in the absence of the proper administrative authorities, to occupy such offices," to direct their minds to the study of law, offering as an inducement a microscopic addition to their pay for proficiency in the subject.

It needed only this to drive Bones into the glad and welcoming arms of the Medicine Hat College of Law and

Jurisprudence, whose page advertisement filled every magazine of note.

"Learn Law!" said the announcement peremptorily.

Bones wrote for information and had back a carload of literature, a letter that began "Dear Friend," and a blank which wasn't a blank at all, and only required his signature on the dotted line to bring the revealed mysteries of the law to his breakfast table.

"And what value the laws of the United States will be to you, God knows," said Hamilton, finding his subordinate immersed in the study of Impersonation. "What you should get down to is an analysis of the ten commandments."

Bones stretched back in his chair wearily and closed his eyes.

"Dear old sir," he said with offensive patience, "why blither? This sort of thing is a bit deep for you, dear old sir. I'll bet that you don't know that it's illegal to pretend you're somebody else?"

"You stagger me," said Hamilton.

"And I'll bet you don't know, poor old ignoramus, that if I went to you an' said I'm Sanders, and I wasn't Sanders, an' you thought I was Sanders an' gave me a cheque, what I should be?"

"I know what I should be," replied Hamilton.

At a later period of the day he expressed his uneasiness to Sanders.

"I've never known Bones to take study quite so seriously," he said. "He's walking about like a man in a dream, and calls me 'your honour.' Do you mind going through the mail, sir, and taking out any correspondence marked 'Medicine Hat School of Law'?"

Sanders smiled.

"I'm afraid I can't do that," he said, "but I'll talk to Bones."

Before he could do so, a curious thing occurred. The corporal of the guard reported that he had seen Bones walking about the parade-ground in the middle of the night. Bones had his hut on the other side of the parade, directly opposite the guard-room, and it was not unusual on a hot night, when sleep was difficult, for the sentry to see a tall young man, in violently striped pyjamas and mosquito boots, pacing up and down outside the house. When the sentry saw the figure in pyjamas walk across to the store-house, an ugly little tin building where the soldiers' clothing was kept, he thought nothing of it. He mentioned the matter to the corporal of the guard, who as casually told Hamilton.

"What time was this?" asked the interested captain of Houssas.

"Lord, it was the third hour before the light."

When they met at breakfast:

"What the devil were you doing in the middle of the night?" asked Hamilton.

"Me, sir?" said Bones. "Sleepin', sir; that's what I generally do, dear old Ham."

Hamilton looked at him in astonishment.

"But, my dear man, you were wandering about the parade-ground at 3 a.m.!"

Bones gaped at him.

"Me, sir? I, sir, I mean? Give the poor old captain a little air," he said gently. "Sun, dear old sir—heat, poor old captain——"

"Do you mean to tell me that you weren't walking around in your impossible pyjamas at three o'clock this morning?"

"No, sir," said Bones. "And as to my pyjamas——"

"We won't discuss those at breakfast," said Hamilton.

"Have you ever walked in your sleep, Bones?" asked Sanders.

"As a youth, sir," admitted Lieutenant Tibbetts; "many, many years ago."

When they discussed the matter in private, Sanders made light of the incident.

"He is working hard, and that probably accounts for

his sleep-walking. He can't do much harm to himself, but you had better tell the sergeant of the guard to keep an eye on him."

That night nothing happened, but on the night following Hamilton, finding the night too hot for sleep, pulled his camp bed on to the stoep, hoping that the mosquitoes would not observe the absence of a protective net. After an hour of slapping and whisking, he rose with a curse, went into the dark dining-room and mixed a tepid lime-juice swizzle. When he came out to his bed, he was as wide awake as ever he had been in his life and, abandoning his plan to re-erect a mosquito net around his bed, sat down in one of the long-seated chairs and lit a cheroot.

There was a full moon—it was almost as light as day. He saw the glitter of the sentry's bayonet as he strolled leisurely up and down, and the dull-red glow of the illicit cigarette which the soldier was smoking. Hamilton grinned. In his early days he would have pulled up the man before him and punished him for this dereliction of duty, but he had learned that there were certain breaches of military law that were so human that to check them arbitrarily was to be guilty of inhumanity.

And then suddenly he saw a pyjama'd figure cross the square and disappear into the hut occupied by Bones. He waited for five minutes and, his curiosity getting the better of him, he got up and, finding an electric torch, walked across the campus. Bones had left both windows and doors wide open and, flashing the rays of his lamp inside, he saw his subaltern lying fast asleep under the mosquito netting. As the light touched his face Bones grunted, turned over. . . .

"Arson," he muttered, "is a form of crime jolly well abhorrent to civilised communities."

Hamilton passed across the square to the sentry, whose cigarette lay glowing on the ground, mute evidence of his offence.

"No, lord, I did not see Tibbetti come out of his little house," said the man; "but there is a door behind where I cannot see, and Tibbetti comes and goes—therefore I did not challenge him, for he is a high one."

"Did he throw away this cigarette?" demanded the sarcastic officer.

"Lord, he must have done this, for who else would smoke?"

Hamilton thought it unwise to discuss the point. On the following day the homeward and outward mails arrived, and amongst the letters (which included fat envelopes from the Medicine Hat School of Law) was the official order to transfer Bugler Achmet to Headquarters. Hamilton had just time to set the man's papers in order (for a soldier is attached to an extensive documentation) and bundle the man on to the north-bound steamer, and was in consequence so busy that he had no time to question the sleep-walker. Bones, in moments of crisis like these, was the weakest of reeds. He invariably entered a man's crimes on his medical history sheet, and recorded a sore throat on the sheet reserved for a soldier's delinquencies.

The opportunity did not come till very late in the evening.

"Bless my jolly old soul!" said Bones, aghast. "Walking in my sleep—you're pulling my leg, Ham!"

"I wasn't near enough to do that, or I'd have given you a spank that would have awakened you."

"And probably killed me!" said the indignant Bones. "That's homicide, dear old officer, in the third degree. Never do that, Ham. Restrain yourself."

So far from being alarmed at this revelation of his eccentricity, Bones seemed rather proud of his abnormality; spoke of hair-raising adventures in his youth, and told a long and thrilling story of how he once walked along a parapet.

"Destruction, dear old sir, staring me in the face."

"I sympathise with destruction," said Hamilton coldly; "but for the moment I warn you that you'll be getting yourself into serious trouble. It wouldn't look well if I appointed a keeper——"

"I should say it wouldn't!" snapped Bones.

"But," continued Hamilton, "you'll have to find some way of stopping this night-prowling of yours. I am going to suggest that you cover your floor with tintacks."

Bones made gurgling noises of protest.

"Or else that you tie your big toe to the bedpost. You're demoralising the detachment, and it has got to be stopped."

Bones shrugged his shoulders.

"I'll look into the matter, sir," he said peevishly.

When he went back to his hut, Fahmeh, the Kano woman, was unrolling his netting and tucking the loose ends under the mattress.

"Now my heart is happy, Tibbetti," she said, "for Achmet has gone on the big ship, and I shall not see him any more."

Bones was not in the mood to gossip about Achmet and the rights and wrongs of this young lady. But he was anxious to secure outside information about his own nocturnal habits.

"Tell me, Fahmeh," he said, "do the soldiers ever see me walking at night?"

To his amazement she nodded.

"Yes, lord, I have seen you in your fine silk bedclothes and your high yellow boots. Once you came to my hut and called my husband, and I came out to you and you told me that you needed him. Because you looked strangely, lord, I thought you were mad."

Bones sat down heavily upon the nearest chair.

"Bless my life!" he said feebly, and turned pale. "Heavens alive and holy snakes!" he added, and ran his fingers through his thin yellow hair.

"Also," she went on remorselessly, "many of the soldiers have seen you go into the house of cloths; and last night Militini saw you."

Bones waved her out of the hut. Perhaps he was going mad? Young men—intelligent and bright young men— had been driven mad before in this territory by the blazing sun and the everlasting blueness of the skies.

When he went up to dinner he carried with him a document, which he thrust tragically before Sanders's eyes.

"I'd like you to witness this, dear old sir an' Excellency," he said miserably. "I've left you my little bungalow at Shoreham, and I've given old Ham all my guns and things . . ."

"What is this?" asked Sanders, examining the document, which began:

I, Augustus Tibbetts, Lieutenant of King's Houssas, being of sounde mind and in full posesion of my fackiltys . . .

"A will? What rubbish! And besides, Bones," smiled Sanders, "I couldn't witness a will that left me even a Shoreham bungalow. Are you feeling ill?"

"No, sir—on the borderline, sir," said Bones, in his most sepulchral tone. "Nutty, sir." He tapped his head. "Seein' things, sir, an' hearin' things, sir, and sky-hootin' all over the place at night, sir."

"Oh, you're sleep-walking? Well, that's not going to kill you," said Sanders and, as Achmet's successor sounded the officers' mess call: "Sit down and eat."

The huts of the Houssas form two lines nearly parallel with the shore of the river. By their side, and nearer to the sea, are their gardens, where sweet potatoes and onions and mealies grow in plenty. At night-time there is a certain picturesqueness about the lines, for three fires burn and there comes the sound of a tuneless banjo, the clapping of hands and the tum-tum of an elongated dancing-drum.

That night, before he went to bed, Bones fixed an elaborate trap calculated to wake him in the event of his taking an unconscious stroll. It consisted of an old shotgun resting precariously on the open edge of the door, and a broom-handle, the requisite height being secured by balancing the broom-handle on a chair.

The man who came to rouse him in the dark hours may have guessed this—a likely possibility, since every man, woman and child in the station had seen Bones fixing the trap.

"Tibbetti!" he called urgently.

At the third repetition of his name Bones leapt out of bed, thrust open the door, and was knocked almost senseless by the shot-gun.

"Man, why do you call me?" he growled, rubbing his head.

"Lord, will you come and see? Benabdul has been killed!"

Bones struggled into his coat, pulled on his boots and went out into the black night.

"Who killed this man?" he asked.

"Lord, none knows. In the night his wife heard him cry out, and when she went from her hut, there, by the favour of God, lay Benabdul."

Somebody had roused a fire to a blaze. All the Houssa huts had emptied, and a crowd of half-naked men and women surrounded the thing on the ground.

The man had been speared through the heart, and lay on his side, his two arms outstretched towards the village street. Benabdul's weeping wife had begged that he be carried into the hut, but the Houssas had left him where they found him.

Bones went up to the Residency and aroused the Commissioner and Hamilton, and together they went back to the huts.

Sanders was puzzled. There was no war in the country, and this man had been so extremely insignificant that he had no enemies except Achmet, who was on a ship and a hundred miles away. Moreover, there were no family quarrels such as distinguish most family circles; he lived happily with his wife and seldom beat her. The thing was inexplicable.

5

Later, Sanders examined the weapon—a short throwing spear. There were scores of them at Headquarters. The Houssas bought or stole them from the Upper River— Bones had a dozen in his own hut.

"It is very queer. Bring the woman to me," he said.

Her friends had succeeded in quietening the sobbing wife, and she was brought to where Sanders sat by the side of the fire.

"Now tell me, woman," he said kindly, "did you hear no sound in the night?"

She hesitated.

"Lord, I heard a voice calling my husband, and he went out," she sobbed.

"What voice?" asked Sanders gently. "For, Fahmeh, you know all your husband's comrades."

She shook her head.

"It was none of these." And then she looked strangely at Bones, and he went as white as death.

"Mine?" he croaked.

She nodded.

"Lord, it was your voice I heard, speaking to my husband," she said in a hushed tone. "And then I heard no more till he cried out."

Bones did not flinch. He grew a little stiffer, a little more erect than usual, then, stooping, picked up the spear which had been taken out and examined it in the light of the fire. One end had been shaved, and there was an initial.

"This is my spear," he said simply. "I brought it down from the N'gombi three months ago."

Hamilton took his hands and turned them over. There was blood on them, but that may have come from the spear he had been handling, which was still wet. And then he turned his cold eyes on Fahmen.

"Woman," he said, "you could not have heard Tibbetti. That is foolish talk. Whilst Tibbetti slept, I sat in the shadow of his hut and watched, knowing his strange way of walking when he sleeps."

"As to that, lord, I know nothing," she said simply, "only it was Tibbetti's voice which called Benabdul into the open."

And she would not budge from this. The sentry was questioned; he had not seen Bones cross the square, but there was a path through the bush, which would have made it possible for him to reach the hut unseen.

"We'll talk this over," said Sanders calmly. "Come up to the house, Bones, and have a drink."

The three men went silently across the square into the dark house, and Hamilton lit the lamps and placed a large bottle of whisky on the table. Bones's face was white and set; he pushed aside the glass with a shake of his head.

"No, thank you, dear old Ham," he said, a trifle huskily. And then: "Did I kill this unfortunate beggar? I must confess that I was thinking about him when I went to sleep."

"You killed nobody," said Hamilton savagely. "What are you blathering about? The woman's half mad with horror, and she'll tell a different story in the morning. Somebody had a grudge against Benabdul and settled him. There's nothing remarkable about that?" he challenged Sanders.

"Nothing," said Sanders quietly.

"Do you think I killed him, sir?" asked Bones, his face tense.

Sanders's hand went up to his chin.

"Do I think you killed him?" he repeated slowly. "No, I don't, Bones."

It was a sleepless night for them all, and when daylight came Sanders had an idea, which he communicated to the senior officer.

"Have you thought of inspecting your store to see if there is anything missing?" he asked. "According to the reports, Bones was seen to visit the store on two different occasions."

The idea had not occurred to Hamilton, and without further ado he found his key and went down to the little

tin building, accompanied by Sergeant Abiboo, that
clerkly man, and made a brief inspection. It was brief
because, at first glance, it was evident that the store had
been visited by somebody in a great hurry. A pile of
brown blankets had been overturned, and when these
were counted six were found to be missing. In the inner
store-room, where preserved foods were kept, a case had
been broken open and ten cans of meat and vegetables had
gone. Nor was this all: in a smaller room of the store—it
was little more than a closet—had been ten stands of new
Lee-Enfield rifles, which had been sent to the station for
tuition purposes, the troops hereabouts being armed with
the old Lee-Metford. Two rifles and a box of ammunition
had disappeared. And, what was more, an attempt had
been made to open the little safe, which, however, contained nothing more valuable than records and stock
sheets.

Hamilton went back to Sanders with the information he
had gleaned.

"A sleep-walker would hardly have made such a syste-
matic robbery," said Sanders thoughtfully. "I'll telegraph
to Headquarters. The boat should have arrived there this
morning, and if the land line's working——"

That it was working, was demonstrated when at that
moment the Eurasian clerk who acted as chief telegraphist
came over with a scrawled message. It was from the
Officer Commanding Troops:

> *Private Achmet was not on ship when arrived. Captain
> believes Achmet jumped overboard before ship left your coast.*

They looked at one another.

"Find Achmet," said Sanders briefly. "He was, I remember, a powerful swimmer, and could easily have
reached the bush."

Behind the beach was a stretch of bush country that ran
for fifty miles northward. It was sparsely inhabited,
being, in certain seasons, subjected to a terrible wind

which invariably missed the river, and except for a few poverty-stricken tribes, who eked out their livelihood by fishing, there were no people of importance in this area.

"He got to the bush, made his way to the station in the night and settled Benabdul," said Hamilton.

"But Bones's voice?" suggested Sanders.

"It is an old trick. These Houssa fellows are born imitators, and Bones is a favourite subject of theirs."

He himself gave a life-like imitation of Bones calling Benabdul in Arabic and by name.

A search of the bush country was impracticable, but Bones and two trackers went along the beach in search of footprints, and two miles from the station they found them, a succession of tracks which led from the sea's edge to the bush, where they disappeared. Just here a shallow stream runs from the bush into the sea, and Bones went up the creek until it got too deep and tangled for wading. Here the crocodiles have a breeding-place, and even as he stepped through the water he heard the splash of a big fellow as it fell from an unseen log into the water.

He returned and reported the tracks. The assembly was sounded; every man, on or off duty, paraded on the square, and one by one Hamilton questioned them. But nobody had seen Achmet, the bugler; and Hamilton knew that they were not lying. The man was not popular and he would find no friends to hide him up.

"You had better sleep at the Residency to-night, Bones," suggested Sanders that evening.

But Bones demurred.

"I want to be sure how much I'm in this, sir," he said quietly. "If old Ham will give orders to the sentry that I'm to be challenged wherever I'm seen, I think I shall be more satisfied."

His eyes were heavy with weariness when he pulled aside the mosquito curtain and lay on the top of his bed that night, and his head had scarcely touched the pillow before he was in a profound sleep.

When he was sure that Bones was slumbering, Hamil-

ton carried a deck-chair down to his hut, planted it outside the door, making a circuit of the hut, and propped a
stout stake against the back door, so that it could not
be opened. When this was done, he returned to the front
of the house, and, settling down with a rug over his
knees, he fell into a fitful sleep. The chair was drawn
across the entrance of the hut so that it was impossible for
anybody to leave without waking him.

The yell that brought him to his feet did not come from
the hut. He stood up, his heart beating a little more
quickly, listening, and heard excited voices coming from
the guard-room. His first thought was of Bones, and,
kicking aside the chair, he ran into the hut—Bones's bed
was empty!

With a sinking heart he ran out and across the square,
just as the sergeant of the guard was setting forth to waken
him.

"Lord," said the man tremulously, "Sergeant Abiboo——"

"Dead?" asked Hamilton, shocked.

"No, lord, but he is hurt. While he slept, somebody
came into his hut and speared him, but he lay on his
side . . ."

Hamilton did not wait for any further information but
flew to the Houssa lines, and, pushing aside the people
who crowded before the entrance of Abiboo's hut, he
went in.

The wound was a slight one. Abiboo was sitting on his
skin bed, whilst one of his two wives dressed the wound
gingerly.

"I know nothing, lord," he said frankly, "except that I
felt this sharp pain and woke up. Before I could get out
of my bed, my enemy had gone."

"Did you hear anybody speaking?" asked Hamilton
quickly.

If Abiboo had not, a woman who slept in the next hut
had heard somebody call him by name.

"It was Tibbetti, lord," she said.

"Mother of fools," snarled Hamilton, "how could it be Tibbetti when Tibbetti is sleeping in his hut?"

Fahmeh detached herself from the group that stood around him.

"Lord, I saw Tibbetti," she said, "walking through the village like a ghost, and carrying in his hand a spear, all red with blood. And this he threw down before my hut, where I sat watching. And because I was afraid I did not touch it."

Sanders had joined them by this time, and the two men went on a tour of inspection. The spear lay in the centre of the pathway which runs between the two lines of huts, and, picking it up, Hamilton turned his light upon the haft and groaned. Without a word he handed the weapon to Sanders.

"Is he in his hut?" asked the Commissioner in a troubled tone.

"No, sir. How he got out, heaven knows!"

The bugler sounded the alarm, and the Houssas hurried into their huts to dress. In parties of twos and threes they were sent out to beat first of all the Residency wood, whilst a stronger party was sent off post-haste along the beach. Throughout the night the search continued, but there was no sign either of Bones or of the Houssa Achmet.

"I can't understand it," said Sanders, when Hamilton returned with the first light of dawn to report the failure of the parties. "Bones could not possibly—pshaw! it's absurd!"

Hamilton stood with his hands clasped behind him, his chin on his breast, a picture of dejection.

"It is horrible," he said, in despair. "Of course, it may be some queer——"

Out of the corner of his eye he saw a man flying across the square. It was the wounded Abiboo. He came up the four steps to the stoep in one leap.

"Master," he said breathlessly, "Fahmeh, the woman of Benabdul, is gone!"

There was a silence.

"Gone?"

The man nodded.

"Yes, lord. Nobody saw her go, but Tibbetti was seen——"

"What!" shouted Hamilton. "When was he seen?"

"When all the men were on the parade-ground," replied the Houssa, "an old woman, who stayed behind because of the swelling in her leg—she was the wife of Corporal Ali Fula, who was killed——"

"Where did she see Tibbetti?" interrupted Sanders.

"In his little ship," was the astonishing answer. "The Chic-a-chic. He passed like a ghost down the stream towards the big waters."

"I'll be damned!" said Hamilton helplessly.

He flew down to the quay, hoping that the woman had been mistaken. The motor-launch was gone.

A first-class mystery this promised to be, and Sanders had written three folios of his report to Headquarters when an excited Hamilton called him to the beach. The little *Wiggle* was coming in from the sea, towing behind a long canoe in which two miserable people were seated.

This was the story of Fahmeh, the Kano woman, when she stood before Sanders:

"Lord, this man Achmet was my lover, because he was young and beautiful and my husband was old and silly. And when Benabdul found me in his arms, I acted as though I hated him, knowing the time would come when we would go away to the Islands of Joy and build a hut and sow our own garden, and live there for ever. And I hated Tibbetti because he sent my man to the dark prison. We had a canoe in the little creek, and, knowing that Tibbetti slept well, Achmet got the key of the house of cloth and took therefrom all we desired for our long journey to the Islands. Also a bag of rice and a bag of salt and lines with cunning hooks for fishing, and cloth to cover us. I killed Benabdul because I hated him, and spoke evilly of Tibbetti because I hated him worse. I would have killed Abiboo for the cruel way he beat my man, but he lay on his side."

Sanders made no comment. It would have been a waste of time. He committed his prisoners to the little lock-up and gave Bones an opportunity of explaining the miracle.

"Thought it all out when I was lying in bed, dear old Excellency," said Bones, "whilst poor old Ham was snoring like a pig outside," he added insolently. "Got the idea in a flash. Deduction an' logic, sir an' brother officer. I knew this naughty old lady had the run of my hut, and was the only person who could take a spear. I'm a very methodical person, dear old sir. A lot of people don't realise that. I knew I had ten, or maybe twelve, spears in my hut, and so I got up, lit the light an' counted 'em, and there were only seven, or maybe nine."

"Or maybe twelve," suggested Hamilton, with a sneer.

"There were three missing, or perhaps five," said Bones gravely. "Anyway, there were some missing. It struck me what a jolly good idea it would be if I went down and searched this wicked old person's hut."

"In the middle of the night," murmured Hamilton.

"I stepped over you, and you never heard me," said Bones in triumph. "And listen, Ham—I'm no sleep-walker! The wicked person who walked in and out of my hut in my pyjamas was Achmet himself. I never dreamt anybody could be such a fearful cad as to pinch my pyjamas. However, that is by the way. I went down to the Houssa lines by the bush path, and I had hardly got into the village when I saw Mrs. Benabdul come out of Abiboo's hut and heard the rumpus. To hide myself was the work of a moment. I guessed the whole story in a second. My brain——"

"We will imagine all that, Bones," said Sanders good-humouredly. "What happened?"

Apparently Bones had followed the murderess through the woods, where her lover was waiting for her with a canoe, provisioned and ready for the journey. The canoe was sliding over the surf before Bones realised the objective of the party, and, dashing back to the quay where the little motor-launch lay, he had set forth in pursuit.

"But I don't walk in my sleep: that's the point I want to make, dear old officer," he said exuberantly. "When I walk I'm awake, and when I'm awake—I'm fearfully keen! If you report this to Headquarters, Excellency"— he addressed Sanders—"you might mention the fact that I did all this without the slightest assistance—in fact, if anything, hampered by my naughty old superior."

Hamilton's reply to this was unprintable.

VIII

THE BALL GAME

DORAN CAMPBELL-CAIRNS was very kind to animals. She adored butterflies, and regarded entomologists who collected them as horrible people. She would not put her dainty foot upon one harmless and necessary worm, and would have swooned at the thought of swatting a fly. She was tall, gloriously slim, had one of those pale, clear complexions that some people find so adorable; beautifully arched eyebrows, and eyes as clear and blue as a morning sky.

She was the only daughter of His Excellency the Administrator, and she had come out for three months, in the healthiest part of the year, before settling in Paris at a finishing school where young ladies are taught the art of dressing, a discriminating taste in operas, all the new dance steps, and are tutored in the ways of most of the old and more expensive restaurants.

She did not seem young to Lieutenant Tibbetts. He thought she was the ideal age. He could not imagine her younger or older. She had fluffy golden hair, and lips calculated to make a susceptible young man dither on his feet. Bones was susceptible and dithered; and the four days that His Excellency spent at the Residency were four coloured plates in his drab book of life; four scented roses in a garden of onions, if so sublime an experience can be likened to anything so ridiculous.

"Bones," said Sanders one morning, "the Administrator is arriving at the end of the week, and he's bringing his daughter with him."

"Bless her jolly old heart!" murmured Bones, immersed for the moment in his mail. "Anything I can do to make the dear old lady comfortable——"

139

"So far as I can remember," broke in Hamilton, knitting his brows in thought, "she's quite a kid. My sister wrote to me about her the other day. She's just left school."

"A few native dolls, I think," said Bones, looking up. "Leave it to me, dear old Excellency. I'll amuse the child. It's a funny thing, dear old Ham, but children take to me. I'm rather like the bagpipe fellow from where-is-it. The moment he tuned up his jolly old pipes—but you've read the novel, dear old Ham: why bother me with questions?"

"To be exact, I haven't asked you a question yet," said Hamilton. "If I did, I should like to know whether you're as big an ass as you seem, or whether this super-ignorance of yours is just show-off."

"Tut tut!" murmured Bones, back again in his correspondence. "Tut tut, dear old baby-snatcher!"

"What you can do," said Sanders, "is to get the tennis net put up, and ask your men to mend the ice plant."

Bones went down to meet the Administrator with a light heart and a whistle. He came back dazed, and, for once in his life, silent.

Miss Doran had naturally attached herself to him because he was the only young man in the party. She thought Sanders looked horribly stern, and confided to the awe-stricken Bones that Hamilton had a cruel mouth.

"Perfectly horrible, young miss," said Bones, hoarse with emotion. "The things that jolly old man says to me——"

"I mean, he looks as if he would—well hurt!"

Bones nodded his head solemnly.

"Simply horrible, dear old young lady," he agreed. "Simply doesn't care a rap for a fellow's feelings."

Those wondrous lips of hers uttered a sound of impatience.

"You're very stupid, Mr. Bones," she said.

"Tibbetts is my name, but you can call me Bones, Miss Excellency," he said.

"I shall call you what I like," replied Miss Excellency tartly.

"And I shall like whatever you call me, dear old person," said Bones, and was so pleased with this reply that he recovered a little of his lost confidence.

Four days of seeing her at breakfast, at tiffin, at dinner! Forty-eight hours of intoxication with her on the *Zaire*, when she went with her father on a little tour of inspection! And the evenings in the dark of the veranda, when she sat in shimmering white, her cool hand so close to his that he could have touched it, and did, in fact, touch it once, explaining hastily that he had brushed off a mosquito. On the fourth morning, in a delirium of misery—for her boat sailed that afternoon—he made a statement.

"The point is, young Miss Doran," he said, in so strange a voice that he did not recognise himself speaking, "I'm simply awfully nutty about you. I am really, dear old miss. I've got an uncle with pots of money—he's an awful big pot—what I mean to say is that he can't live for ever—few people do, dear old miss . . . I know you're very young and I'm simply fearfully old, and your jolly old father's a perfect terror—though we shouldn't see much of him——"

"What on earth are you talking about?" Her starry eyes were fixed on his.

Bones cleared his throat, wiped the perspiration from his damp forehead with a small silk Union Jack, one of his most-prized possessions, which he intended donating before her departure; coughed again, looked everywhere except at her, and then, in a moment of extreme desperation:

"The point is, dear old lady, what about it?" he asked hoarsely.

"What about what?"

"Jolly old matrimony," croaked Bones. "Tum-tum-ti-tum-tum-tum . . ."

She didn't recognise Mendelssohn's Wedding March, but it was well intended.

"Matrimony? Are you proposing to me?" Her eyebrows rose haughtily.

Bones nodded. He was dumb with adoration, fear, hope, and sensibility.

"How perfectly ridiculous!" said this young lady who would not tread on a harmless and necessary worm, or cruelly swat a fly, or pin Purple Emperors to a bit of cork. "How perfectly horribly stupid! I couldn't *possibly* marry you! You're so awfully old. How old are you?"

"A hundred and five," said Bones, in a dismal effort to be jocular.

"I'm sure you're twenty-four if you're a day," she said severely, "and you're awfully plain."

"Me?" said the indignant Bones. "Me plain? Don't be absurd, dear old silly one."

"Of course you're plain!" she scoffed. "Look at your nose!"

Bones squinted down the organ in question, but could see nothing remarkable except that it was a brick-red, but then, so was the rest of his face.

"What's the matter with my nose?" he demanded hotly. "And if it comes to that, you've got no nose worth speaking about."

She opened her mouth in an O of pain and wrath.

"How dare you speak about my nose! I shall tell my father."

"And you jolly well ought to," said Bones bitterly, "because he's partly responsible."

"Oh!" she said again, and then, maliciously: "I couldn't possibly marry a man who isn't an athlete. And if you want to know, I'm in love with Harry Gilde. He's one of the best forwards in the Cambridge pack."

Bones waggled his head impatiently.

"That's the kind of person you would be in love with—a forward! As if you're not forward enough!"

"Let us walk back to the Residency," she said, with ominous calm.

Bones shrugged, and walked by her side.

"After what I have done for you," he said, after a long pause.

She stopped and glared at him.

"What have you done for me?"

"I've shown you everything, haven't I?" he squeaked indignantly. "Who put the tennis net up? I did!"

"And a beastly old tennis net it is," she said.

"It's the best we've got," said Bones quietly.

"What else have you done? Now tell me that!"

Bones couldn't think for the moment, but waved his hand round the landscape.

"Did you make the earth, I wonder?" she asked sarcastically. "Are you the Lord's head gardener?"

It was Bones's turn to be shocked.

"Do not let us discuss it," he said, and with tightly pressed lips they walked back to the Residency.

The Administrator was on the point of departure.

"Where on earth have you been, Doran?" he asked, though very mildly, for he was in some awe of his beautiful daughter.

"I have been seeing"—her tone was very deliberate—"a strange insect, and watching its curious antics," said Doran, glancing sideways at Bones.

"So have I," said he defiantly. "One of the most stuck-up insects . . ."

She took her father's arm and left him so abruptly that it was quite noticeable.

"Are you coming down to the beach, Bones?" asked Hamilton.

His subaltern performed a wonderful grimace in which scorn, indifference, disgusted amusement and superiority to womankind at once fought for expression and suffered defeat. Nevertheless, there were tears in his eyes when he saw the white ship go slowly over the horizon, and a lump in his throat, and a dull, aching pain in the place where his heart had been. He almost wished he could take to drink, but unfortunately whisky made him sick, and he invariably fell asleep after his second glass of port.

"What did you think of her, Bones?" asked Hamilton.

"Not a bad kid," said Bones indifferently. "Rather precocious, but not bad."

"I thought she was beautiful," said Sanders quietly, looking up.

"Ye-es," admitted Bones, "but looks are nothing. Intelligence is everything, dear old Excellency. And, as jolly old Kipling says, I've done this, that and the other, and I've learnt about women from her."

He retired early; refused pointedly Hamilton's invitation to piquet, and spent the greater part of the night writing a poem in the tragic style.

> "You came into my life
> And I asked you to be my little wife.
> But you went and threw my nose into my face.
> But Heaven made us all
> And it made your nose too small
> But I do not consider that a very great disgrace.
>
> "O my heart is sick and empty,
> And soon I'll find a soldier's fate upon a battle-field.
> For when I think of thee,
> Thy lovely figure I'll see,
> And I don't suppose you'll care if I am killed!!
>
> "So let this be a warning
> (What happened the other morning)
> Don't break a heart that beats for thee, my dear.
> You will never see me again.
> I may be very plain,
> But I'm not such a nut as I appear.
>
> "P.S.—I withdraw all remarks about your nose."

This epistle may or may not have reached Miss Doran Campbell-Cairns. If it did come to her hands, she was so overcome by remorse that she hadn't the heart to reply. Whatever was the cause, there was no answer. Bones grew cynical about women and began to read the sporting newspapers, whilst his interest in Rugby football revived.

And then there occurred the incident in the village of Ugundi which caused him to take a close personal interest in a game that he had not played since he was at school.

Near the village of Ugundi is a place which is called the Ten Leopards. It is a spot innocent of shade or herbage, and is surrounded by piles of rotting, fungus-covered tree-trunks which the great elephants, generations ago, tore up for their sport and threw to one side. Even at the river's edge lie these reminders of the big ones' strength and fancy, for blackened boles reach down layer on layer through the sand and mud, and the river has cemented them with silt until they are immovable.

For hundreds of years the elephants came to play on the stark earth, to bellow and trumpet their mock defiance, and to wrestle harmlessly at that season of the year when even the oldest and most irritable of bulls could fight head to head and never be tempted to employ their sharp tusks. Here came the calves in herds, to engage in mimic warfare under the eyes of sleepy cows, and here, on one memorable day, were found the mangled remains of ten leopards. Perhaps they had stalked a calf, for it was the period of famine.* But why ten leopards should be found together (being naturally unsociable) is a mystery which the ages have not solved.

There was a palaver in the near-by village of Ugundi where Mr. Commissioner Sanders sat in judgment on the domestic value of Katabeli, the wife of the Akasava chief and the fourteenth known daughter of the Isisi king.

M'laba, the chief, had purchased this woman, paying three sacks of salt, two rare and precious dogs and four thousand brass rods, which was a very great price for one who was an indifferent dancer. And now M'laba desired the return of the treasure he had paid, for the woman had taken her fancy elsewhere.

Sanders listened with patience to the list of her lovers, known and suspected, dropping, at long intervals, a pungent word or two upon the morals of the Isisi, and at dusk on the third day gave to the husband what was equivalent to a decree *nisi* with the custody of the salt.

Ordinarily such a palaver might have been settled in a

* Sanders put the year at 1763.

day. Unfortunately, there were more than the usual tribal complications, for Katabeli was the daughter of a three-mark chief and his wife, and M'laba was a two-mark-crossways man. In other words, their faces were, in the one case, decorated with three lateral cicatrices, and in the other two in the shape of a St. Andrew's cross. The exact complication may not be patent to the casual observer, but, reduced to practical politics, the marriage had represented first the union between rival races, and secondly that it had united (temporarily) the conflicting interests of the League of Saloon Keepers with the Good Templars. The Isisi and the Akasava were, in fact, incompatible in ethics and concrete practice. And the divorce meant trouble.

"Lord," said the father of the woman, "this is not justice, for my daughter has given this man a son, and that alone entitles her to the salt. Also, these two-mark-cross-ways men will mock me, and my young men will be hard to hold against these haughty Akasava."

"Whoever mocks you mocks me," said Sanders. "And as for the salt and the child, you shall have back as much salt as this child weighs."

And solemnly the little brown-faced imp of a baby was weighed on the big wooden balance against as much salt as turned the scale—after Sanders had removed from the child's little body a belt from which were suspended certain heavy pieces of iron.

"Lord, if these are taken away," said the disgruntled grandfather, "he will have bad luck all his life."

"And if I do not take them away," said Sanders, "you will get too much salt, and that would be bad luck indeed for M'laba."

He left two strong, virile and homicidal people, by no means satisfied with his judgment. And it happened that these two were what he called "key tribes," and had for generations past been prominent factors in the making of war. Between the bloodthirsty Akasava folk and the truculent borderers of the Isisi had been the beginning of many sanguinary conflicts which had involved whole nations. And Sanders went back to Headquarters feeling more than a little uneasy.

The crops had been very good that year, and good crops are the foundation of war. Also, the fish had been abundant in that part of the river, and men had grown wealthy between rain and rain. He was so apprehensive that, half-way to Headquarters, he stopped the *Zaire* and swung the vessel round, intending to go back and devise on the spot some system of permanent conciliation. He thought better of this and resumed his journey. In the first place, his return would be a weakness, and incidentally would add to the importance of the possible contestants.

Bones, about this time, had wearied of correspondence schools and had grown bored to such an extent that he had even spoken slightingly of the newspaper, published in his home town, which invariably printed his contributions, no matter upon what subject. And Bones without a hobby was rather like a sick cow: he brooded and moped, and made low, clucking noises, intended to express his disgust with life and all that life brought to him. But Sanders was too occupied with the menace of war to worry about Bones.

In moments like these he was wont to call a council of himself and his two officers, with Ahmet, his chief spy, in attendance. But since he had left Ahmet behind to gain intelligence, no decision was reached until that incomparable news-gleaner came down the river with his canoe and his hired paddlers, and laid before the Commissioner a direful review of the situation.

"Lord, there will be war," he said; "for the woman and her kinsman are very hurt against M'laba, and in the eyes of her people she is right. This is the way of the Isisi folk, as you know, Sandi: that if a woman goes here or there, there is no scandal about it, because the Isisi think such ways are human. And as your lordship knows, the Isisi men do not put away their women unless they are lazy or cook food so that it hurts a man's inside. I have seen new spears in both villages, and M'laba has sent his headman to the N'gombi country with fish and salt to buy more."

"This war must be stopped," said Sanders, "and stopped without gun-play."

He looked at Bones with a thoughtful eye.

"I have a mind to send you to sit down in the country, Bones," he said. "I think your presence might do a whole lot to stop any trouble. If you can hold them tight till the rains come, there will be no fighting."

Bones had a ready-made scheme, and, to Hamilton's surprise, Sanders accepted it without question and was even mildly enthusiastic.

"It doesn't seem possible that you could get these devils to play Rugger—but they're children. You can try, Bones, but to be on the safe side you had better send for Bosambo—I'll feel happier if you have at your back a few score of Ochori spears."

So Bones went up in the *Zaire* and was deposited near the Place of the Ten Leopards, which is a sort of neutral ground between the Akasava and the Isisi.

He came none too soon, he learned after his tents had been pitched; for whilst his men were making a rough thorn fence to enclose his little camp, Bones strolled into Ugundi and found the young men engaged in warlike exercises, under the admiring eyes of their womenfolk.

The appearance of Bones was unexpected. M'laba, the chief (he was a great chief, for there were two thousand souls in his village), had not overlooked his coming, for the Place of the Ten Leopards was seldom visited.

"This comes about, lord Tibbetti," said M'laba, "because of the pride of my wife and her father. We are also proud people, and *cala cala* it is said that the Akasava ruled the land from the mountains to the great waters."

Bones sat on a carved stool before the chief's hut, and the young men who had been leaping and dancing stood stock-still and looked foolish.

"I like you too well, M'laba, to see you hanging on a

high tree because of such madness," said Bones. "And I have a great thought in my stomach that soon I will hold a palaver in the Place of the Leopards and will tell you what I desire."

He went from there to the Isisi village, which was five miles distant, but here his arrival had been noted. The *Zaire* had passed the village on its way up-stream, and there were no signs of warlike preparations. The women were pounding their corn, and the young men were telling one another dreadful stories about their prowess in other directions than war. But there were certain signs significant to Bones. Katabeli, the divorced wife of the Akasava chief, held an honourable place in the family circle, which is not usual in divorced women; and she wore certain anklets and bracelets of brass about her comely arms, which showed the favour in which she was held.

"We do not think of war," said her old father, the chief, "for that would be an evil against Sandi. But if these dogs of Akasava attack us, we must defend our village because of the women and the children whom they will so cruelly use. Now *cala cala*, Tibbetti, it is said that the Isisi ruled this country from the Ghost Mountains . . ."

Bones listened patiently, and in the end made a date for a palaver, choosing a time that would allow his most valuable ally to come on the spot.

Bosambo, summoned by pigeon, brought three canoes, each controlled by twenty paddlers, who became warriors by the simple process of exchanging their paddles for spears and shields the moment they touched land. After the first greetings Bones explained his high intention, and the two villages were called to a palaver and ordered to leave their spears behind them.

They sat, the Akasava to his left, the Isisi on his right, and between them the solid phalanx of Ochori spearsmen, Bosambo squatting at their head, and half a dozen yards from Bones.

As a native orator Lieutenant Tibbetts had few equals. He spoke the Bomongo tongue more fluently than Sanders, and he had at his finger-tips all the familiar imagery of the river.

"Listen, all people," said Bones. "I will tell you of a magic which has made my country great. For my people do not fight in anger; they strive against one another with a good heart, and whosoever wins in this striving receives a high reward. Now I want from you, chiefs of the Aka-sava, and you, chiefs of the Isisi, fifteen strong men, very supple and wonderfully fleet of foot. And thus we shall do . . ."

To translate the theory and practice of Rugby football into Bomongo was something of an accomplishment, and Bones succeeded so well that men who had come with murder in their hearts went away with no other thought than this magic of bloodless fighting.

It was a great day for Bones, for towards evening came a paddler from Headquarters, bringing a letter from Sanders, and, miracle of miracles! a large square envelope inscribed in huge letters: "Lieutenant Tibbetts, King's Housas." Instinct would have told him the sender's name even if he had not her signature, in large and flamboyant handwriting, in his autograph book.

Dear Mr. Tibbetts (said the letter), *I am simply Fear-fully Thriled with your Poem! How wonderfully clever you must be! I feel I have been a perfect Pig to you! Will you ever forgive me? I think your Nose is very hansome! It reminds me so much of dear Napoleon Boneypart's! Do please write! I shall be here for another month.*

Bones wrote. He gave in outline the scheme he had in his mind. He hinted darkly of the terrible danger in which he stood. He spoke with bitter self-reproach of his own "boreishness" and hoped she was quite well, as he was at present.

The work of coaching the rival teams went on week after week. At first there were certain difficulties, but they were difficulties of enthusiasm rather than of technique; for both Isisi and Akasava took most kindly to the game.

"Yesterday," said an Akasava forward, "when we laid our heads together for the little ball to be put under our feet, an Isisi dog pinched me behind. Now to-day I am taking a little knife. . . ."

Fortunately Bones discovered the "little knife" before the next scrum was formed, and kicked the enthusiastic player round the plain of the Ten Leopards, which was their practice ground.

Tackling led to a little unpleasantness.

"O man," said the exasperated trainer, "if, when you catch the runner with the ball, you bite him on the leg, I will beat you till you are sore!"

"Lord," pleaded the delinquent, "when I threw this man down I fell upon him, and he was so easy to bite."

Bosambo of the Ochori was a fascinated observer of these strange happenings.

"Lord, this game is like war without spears," he said. "Now what will be the end of it?"

Bones explained his scheme. He would have a match before the spectators of both villages, who were now rigorously excluded from viewing the proceedings; and it would be agreed that whichsoever tribe was vanquished should accept defeat. The season was progressing; the rains were near at hand, and the murmur of war had sunk down so that it was so faint a whisper that it could not be heard in either camp.

Sanders's approval was a great asset to the young man, but the first joy was the scrawled letter and the little wooden box which came up with the Commissioner. Doran Campbell-Cairns was just on the point of departure from the coast.

I think you are simply wonderful (she said). *Do write to me in Paris* (she gave no address). *Papa thinks your skeme of Rugger is simply wondirful! I am sending you a cup which I bought out of my own pocket-money. It isn't really gold, but daddy says the gold will not wear off for years. Do please forgive me all I said about your Nose.*

Bones would have forgiven her anything, and when, later, she became engaged to the son of a lordly house he forgave her that.

The cup was a magnificent one.

"It might," said Bones, in an awe-stricken voice, "have cost a hundred!"

Later he found the label on the base and was considerably surprised that so rare and gorgeous an article could be sold at so small a price.

On the morning of the match Sanders presided at the great palaver, and the atmosphere was almost genial.

"You really are a remarkable fellow, Bones," he said to the smirking young man. "And thank God the glass is going down!" he added inconsequently.

All the Akasava people within fifty miles, all the Isisi within eighty, were assembled on that great plain. They covered the branches of trees; they were massed on the gentle slope that goes up to the Isisi woods; for in this natural amphitheatre the lot of the sightseer was an easy one.

"Too many for my liking, and mostly men," said Sanders, glancing round.

He sat before a little tent in a space apart from the people, and before him, on a table, was the cup of gold that glittered in the dull rays of the sun that shone through watery clouds.

He sent his soldiers amongst the people to look for arms, but apparently they carried nothing more lethal than their long walking-poles. The match began in tropical heat, and when Bones blew his whistle and the Isisi pack leapt forward, there was such a roar, such a quiver of excitement amongst the sightseers, that the thrill of it communicated itself to Sanders.

To his amazement he found he was watching a very good second-rate ball game. The forward work was extraordinarily skilful; the scrums expeditiously formed and dispersed. It was when L'mo, a tall Akasava man, tackled an Isisi forward and brought him smashing to the ground and knelt on his shoulders, that the trouble really started. Two grave spectators leapt out of the press and smote L'mo on the head. But even this incident was adjusted and the game went on.

The first penalty goal was kicked against the Isisi, amidst roars of approval from the unthinking Isisi onlookers. It was L'mo who caused the second incident. Again he tackled, again he brought down his man, but, not content with wrenching the ball from his grip, he took the unfortunate forward by the ears and was dragging him into the middle of the field when Bones interfered.

Play went on for two minutes, possibly less. And then an Akasava back leapt upon an unfortunate rival who was carrying the ball by his teeth, and slowly and scientifically began to strangle him. The crowd broke.

"Back!" roared Sanders.

Bones flew to the thin line of Houssas and the solid square of Bosambo's warriors.

"No spears, thank God!" said Sanders.

Before him was a multitude of waving sticks. Little fights were going on all over the ground. Groups of Akasava men were at grips with the Isisi.

"Fix bayonets!" said Bones breathlessly, and into the battling throng the bright bayonets made their way, until the howling, fighting multitude were divided into two unequal portions.

And at that moment the blessed rain began to fall, not in dainty showers, but in a torrential waterspout that burst suddenly from the grey heavens. Bosambo's men were clearing the ground left and right, but there was no necessity. The villagers were streaming homeward, nursing their wounds and howling their tribal songs.

"That lets us out," said Sanders.

He looked round to where the table had been that held the magnificent prize, but the table was a mass of splintered wood and the cup had disappeared.

"I hope the winner got it," said Sanders, with a grim smile. "By the way, who won?"

Bones was unable to supply the information, but had he been in the waterlogged canoe of Bosambo, as it made its way through the slack waters towards the Ochori country, he would not have been at a loss. Bosambo brought to Fatima, the sunshine of his soul and his one wife, a lovely gold cup.

"This Sandi gave me because of my strength and cleverness in a game which Tibbetti has taught the nations, and in which I alone excel. From this I will drink the beer you brew for me, O dove and light of my eyes!"

IX

THE WISE MAN

At rare intervals, once in a hundred years or so, there arise from a crowd of charlatans and make-beliefs, magicians of such potency that they are remembered when the names of kings and chiefs are forgotten. Some such, by the accident of nature, die in their youth and their powers are unknown. Others reach maturity and find no call for their gifts, or jealously preserve the secrets from their neighbours. Others are misunderstood and pass almost automatically into the category of madmen.

But T'chala, the wise man of the Ochori, had a middle course steered for him, for he was the only son of a man rich in stock and salt and brass rods, which are the currency of this part of the world; and because he loved his fellows and did harm to none, and, if he could not prophesy benevolently, would not prophesy at all, he approached the status of holiness, and even Sanders, who looked slantwise at all men who claimed to be supernaturally gifted, and had a rope or a set of shackles for any who used their reputation evilly—even Sanders spoke fairly to him, and never visited the Upper Ochori but he called at the wise man's hut and listened to his philosophy.

"What strange things do you see, T'chala?" he once asked.

"Lord, in the night I see the dead," said T'chala. "They pass me from left to right, a crowd of faces, black and white and yellow, and I am not afraid, because they are real, for death is reality and life is a sick man's dream."

"What else?" asked Sanders.

"Lord, certain things come at my command and speak to me. But that is mad talk, and you will put me with the old men on the island, where my brother has gone."

"What do they say to you?" asked Sanders patiently.

T'chala brooded a moment, his chin on his palm, and then:

"They tell me that the first thing in all the world is truth," he said, "and that all evil grows out of the seed of a lie—wars and killings and pain and death."

"And do you see M'shimba-M'shamba and a little green lizard?" asked Sanders artfully.

T'chala smiled.

"That is the great folly of the world," he said, "that people make their gods in the shape of men and the things they fear. This is my great thought, that gods do not live or hide in the earth or in the sky or in the deep waters, but that the earth lives in the gods. Now, Sandi, you will say I am mad."

Sanders laughed softly.

"I think you are very wise, T'chala," he said; "wiser than many wise men I know."

He gave the man salt and a can of preserved fruit, to which he was very partial.

Soon after this T'chala fell sick of a fever, and because of his great holiness and association with devils the people of his village, who loved him, concluded it was best to let him die, for fear they offended his many deities and familiars by feeding him. So they left him without meat or drink, and he would certainly have joined the procession which passed his eyes every night, only the wife of a chief, M'lema, out of a fit of contrariness and because of her hauteur, carried him food and drink and brought him back from the land of ghosts.

This M'lema was one of two sisters in the Ochori country, being the daughter of the oldest wife of a common man who was called N'kema—as all common men are called. M'lema, the elder sister, was tall and beautiful by the peculiar standards of the land, and O'fara, the younger, was neither tall nor beautiful, so that she was glad to marry an elderly fisherman who had his lonely hut on the edge of the shallow lagoon which was called

The Beard because of the rushes and grasses that bristled on its surface.

She satisfied all the marital requirements of this old man, and these may be stipulated. She dried and smoked the fish he caught; she soaked and pounded manioc for his bread; she attended the garden where his mealies grew, and cooked for him his morning and evening meals. He was too old a man for love, yet strong enough to wield a stick when she failed him; for he thought that after a time she would be content to be left alone and count herself fortunate when she did not attract his attention.

O'fara thought the matter out for the greater part of a year, and then she found sympathy in a woodman who was young and glad to be alive. In due course the matter came before the chief of that district, a rich man who had married O'fara's sister. There was no defence, as they say in more civilised communities. O'fara came to the palaver carrying all the evidence on her hip, and the old fisherman provided details to the accompaniment of uproarious laughter, for the Ochori people are a cannibal stock, and cannibals laugh very easily. In the end the chief gave divorce; and since there was no wedding portion to restore, nobody suffered but O'fara.

When she went to her rich sister, M'lema showed her the way past the fire, as the saying is.

"You have brought great shame upon me and my man," she said, in so loud a voice that the evidence straddling O'fara's hip opened its sleepy eyes and surveyed his aunt solemnly. "You are an evil woman and there is no place for you in my hut."

So O'fara went to the woods and slept in an old hut that had once held a dead man and was therefore abandoned, and here she lived and her child learned to walk. She had some skill with the line, and in the dark of night caught fish, till the fishermen found her. She ran fast enough from them, but one fleeter than the rest kept on her heels as she doubled hither and thither, and ran her to bay on the banks of the river.

"Now, woman," he said, "I know what devil has frightened away the fish from the river, so that I and my brothers must go to the Isisi country before we make a catch."

He tied her wrist and ankle (she was too winded to struggle) and by this time the other fishermen came up, and after each man had beaten her with his leather girdle, they had a conference in the early light of morning as to what should be done with her. The delay was fatal to any plan, for round the bluff came the white hull of the *Zaire*, the blue ensign with the golden crown drooping over the threshing stern-wheel. And Sanders, who had wonderful eyes, and a more wonderful pair of prismatic glasses, saw the group and sent the shallow boat into the bank.

"Lord, this woman frightened away the fish in the river; and she is evil, for when she was the wife of K'raviki, the fisherman, she did so-and-so and so-and-so."

"O, ko!" said Sanders, politely amazed.

O'fara got up to her feet stiffly, feeling her hurts.

"Tell me, man," said Sanders to the chief fisherman, "how many times did you beat this woman?"

The uneasy little headman hazarded a guess.

"That number of times you shall be beaten, and as many again," said Sanders gently.

He snapped two fingers, and Sergeant Abiboo took off his coat and rolled up his sleeves. . . .

Sanders went into the forest where the woman's child was and took them back to the *Zaire*. An hour later he saw the chief of the big village where was O'fara's sister, so encumbered with brass anklets and bangles that she rattled as she walked.

"Chief, I see you," Sanders greeted him, and took and tasted the salt that the man held in the hollow of two hands. "I bring you this woman and this child. She shall sit down in your village and no man shall harm her."

The chief was not pleased; his wife, less in awe of a man, was shrill.

"O'fara is a scandalous woman," she said; "and Sandi

does not know that when she was the wife of K'raviki the fisherman . . ."

Sanders saw the approving nods of the women.

"Bring me a bowl of goat's milk," he said; and, when it was brought: "Let any wife drink of this," he said, "and if she has no lover but her husband, the milk will stay white; but if she has a lover it will turn black."

M'lema's hand was half-way out—but now it drew back.

"Lord, this is magic, and I am frightened," she whimpered.

Sanders held the bowl towards the awe-stricken audience, but the women shrank away. A sardonic smile broke upon his face.

"O virtuous wives!" he mocked. "Who is there virtuous here?"

The wide-eyed baby on O'fara's hip made a little sound, and Sanders held the bowl to its lips.

"White—it remains," he said; "for this one has no sin."

He looked straightly at the chief.

"What shall I do with O'fara?" he asked; and M'lema's husband, with a face like thunder, answered:

"Let her stay, lord Sandi; by my head and life she shall be safe. As to my wife, I know what I know—but I shall know more."

Again the cold eyes met his.

"In a moon I come to you for a palaver, chief. I would have you sitting by my side; but if you sit before me, I shall do justice."

A sufficient warning for Sabaya, who contented himself with the use of an admonitory stick.

That night, when her husband had gone with his men to the woods to shoot monkeys, M'lema met her lover, a young man to whom she was as a god. He was an Akasava man and familiar with holy things, for he was missionary-trained and had met M'lema in the days when he was a lay preacher—which was before Father Beggelli found him out.

"Go secretly to-night," she said, "to T'chala, the wise man, who lives at the very end of the village. And because he loves me—for when he was sick I went to him and gave him food and goat's milk—he will do many things for me. Tell him that Sandi has shamed me because of my sister, O'fara, and he must put a magic upon O'fara so that she withers up and grows old and dies, she and the child of the woodman."

Bologa, the Akasava man, was alarmed.

"That is a bad palaver," he said. "Let the woman stay, for she will be taken on a blessed day when the sheep and the goats are divided—this the God-man told us."

The woman did not urge him; she ordered, and obediently the lover went to the hut of T'chala and found him sitting before his door in the cool of the evening, with a far-away look in his eyes, for he was thinking of truth.

He listened whilst Bologa spoke in his roundabout way, and all the time T'chala's face was immobile and expressionless. Presently the lover came back to where he had left the woman.

"This man is mad," he said, "for he talked only of truth and of lying, and when I asked him if he would do this thing, he said it was evil, and evil was not for such a man as he."

"Go back to this old dog," said M'lema urgently, "and tell him that when Sandi comes he must say no word of what you have said. I wish I had left him to die."

Bologa returned to the hut of the wise man and delivered his message.

"If he asks me I must speak," said T'chala simply. "For a lie is like the little snake that breaks in two and becomes two snakes, so that, if they are not killed, all the world crawls with them."

M'lema, in a panic, could think of only one solution to her problem. In the middle of the night, when T'chala slept, the lover, who was a member of the Yellow Ghosts, went down to the river, to the place where the clay was, kneaded a large lump and, creeping into the old man's hut, pressed it over his face, and lay upon him for a reasonable time, until his spasmodic jerkings grew still. And that, thought M'lema, was the end of wisdom. Yet, when she went out in the morning, expecting to find a crowd of mourners about the hut, there, in the morning sunlight, sat T'chala, his hands clasped before him, his far-away eyes fixed upon truth.

The lover, grey with fear, heard the news, and would have fled into the forest, only there came word from T'chala that he had need of the man; and he went fearfully.

"Bologa, I see you," said T'chala gravely. "But because of your evil no other man shall see you from this day."

Bologa, sick with terror, walked back along the village street, and came to a family group where his brother sat.

"O, ko!" he said. "A terrible thing has happened to me."

But his brother did not look up or answer, and nobody in the village seemed conscious of his presence. He stooped down and touched the shoulder of the man, but his hand had no weight or substance. He screamed aloud in his fear, but nobody heard him.

"O people, listen!" he shrieked. . . .

Not a head turned.

Frantically he flew along the village street and saw M'lema sitting alone before her hut, watching a boiling pot.

"M'lema," he whimpered, "the old man has put his magic upon me."

She neither raised her eyes nor her head, and when, with a howl of fear, he gripped her arm, his hands closed on nothing.

This was the story he told when they brought him to the little island.

"And the curious thing was," said Sanders, when the story came round to him, "that all the people who saw Bologa swear that he did not move from the front of T'chala's hut, but that he sat there for the greater part of

6

an hour. Undoubtedly he was mad when they took him away. You might look him up the next time you go to the Ochori, Bones, and see if you can get sense out of him."

When old or young men went silly, it was the custom, from time immemorial, to put out their eyes, if they were not already blind, and lead them to a place convenient for the prowling leopards; and when Mr. Commissioner Sanders checked this practice, there were many old people, though they might themselves be the sufferers in a few years' time, who protested bitterly against this unwarrantable interference with the liberty of the subject.

Bosambo of the Ochori governed his country with a rod of iron, and woe to those who broke the law he gave! For he was a very fast walker and could outpace the longest-legged soldier of his country; and always he carried his wicker shield and the six little throwing-spears that never failed to get home. And when he passed on the word of his master, that the old way with the aged was taboo, young men grumbled and obeyed.

A new method was found for disposing of aged relatives. A tiny village was built for them on a broad peninsula that jutted out into the river, and which was connected to the shore by a narrow strip of land. Every morning, men appointed for the purpose brought food for the silly folk, and a guard was set on the isthmus to prevent the decrepit ones from reaching the mainland. It was a good scheme and was born in the fertile mind of Lieutenant Tibbetts of the King's Houssas. But it had this disadvantage over the earlier method: that it gave crazy people an opportunity of meeting one another and of discussing their pet abominations. By common consent they fixed upon a lanky youth who wore a monocle, even in his sleep.

"This man," said Bologa, a mere stripling, but, by reason of his magical experience, a person of importance, "has treated us cruelly, for he has put us in prison. Now in the days of my father we sent old men into the forest, where they were free, and we made it so that they could not see the terrible beasts that prowl at night."

His hearers agreed. There were seven old men and Bologa sitting in a semicircle around a large fire, and they had fed well: the Government was generous, and some of them had relatives who brought them food. They talked aimlessly about Bones far into the night. Two of the old men fell asleep; two were heavily engaged in conversation with the invisible spirits that visited them; but the other three listened eagerly.

"You are old and weak; he is young and strong. And am I not strong also? And shall not the strength of eight little dogs pull down a leopard?"

With some difficulty they awakened the two sleepers and told them of their plan, which, briefly, was to catch Bones on one of his visits, overpower him, and deal with him in six various ways, for each of the old men had his own pet idea. It might have gone out of their crazy minds, but unfortunately Bones came on the morrow, a smirk on his angular face, his large monocle reflecting the light of the westering sun.

"Ah, there you are, you jolly old souls!" said Bones, who came quite alone, having left the *Zaire* at a wooding three miles away. "Happy and content and full of beans!"

The guard at the far end of the isthmus had not been on duty when he passed; had, in point of fact, been to a wedding feast at the village, and he neither saw the young man come nor go.

The first intimation of danger came when a thin and wiry arm was flung round Bones's neck and two knobbly knees were pressed suddenly into his back. Had it been in the open, the thing could have been seen; but he was in the common hut inspecting the arrangements he had made for their comfort.

And here Bones might have ended his career in a most unpleasant manner; but there happened along the great war-craft of Bosambo, king of the Ochori, and the chant of his paddlers reached the ears of the crazy men, and, childlike, they abandoned their task and went to the edge of the water to watch the wonderful canoe with its banging drums and its scarlet awning (once the curtain dividing Sanders's sleeping-cabin from his workroom) and clap their hands in time to the magnificent rhythm of twenty-four paddlers dipping their scarlet blades into the water like one.

Bosambo would have gone past, only he saw that all the crazy men were armed. His canoe swung in and he leapt lightly ashore.

"O ghost men, what is this?" he asked.

"Lord Bosambo," said Bologa, "we have Tibbetti in that hut and we are going to do so-and-so and so-and-so."

And the other seven nodded and repeated each his own formula.

In three strides Bosambo was in the hut, had cut the cord about the neck of the choking young man, and had hauled him into the daylight.

"Lord, what shall I do with these old fools and the young fool who is most foolish of all?" he asked. "They are crazy and are better dead. Now, if you say the word, I will ask them to come into the great hut, and as each man enters he will die and never know."

"You're a wicked old murderer!" said the indignant Bones, and Bosambo beamed.

"I be Christian man same like Marki-Luki-Johnni," he said, "I go heaven one-time, you go heaven one-time, howdjedo!"

He gave a passable imitation of himself welcoming Bones to a better world.

Bones had had a scare: one of the worst that had ever come to him, for there was an eerie ugliness about this danger which left a deeper impression upon his mind than other and worse perils.

All the way to Headquarters he pondered on the most acceptable reward he could offer to Bosambo. The chief, whom he had consulted, was frankness itself.

"Lord, give me money," he said, "for every time I see

the great king's face upon a silver coin, my heart grows very strong for him."

But Bones had other views.

"Why not," suggested his cynical superior (and Captain Hamilton could be very cynical indeed), "why not an illuminated address? Or a set of fish-knives? Or a marble clock with or without gilt angels?"

"Don't let us drag in religion, dear old sir," begged Bones gravely. "Let us keep our naughty old minds in the strait an' narrow, dear old agnostic. Bosambo—by gum!"

He slapped his palm with a skinny fist, and in another second had leapt down the steps of the Residency and was flying across the sun-baked parade-ground. In a little time he returned, flushed of face and smirking; under each arm he carried a thick package of magazines. These he laid on the table.

"I know what you're giving him," said Hamilton; "a gramophone— five shillings down and ten shillings a month for the term of your natural life?"

Bones shook his head.

"A correspondence course in salesmanship—sign the blank and send no money?" suggested Hamilton.

"Wrong, old guess-works."

"Wait!" Hamilton clasped his forehead. "It can't be gents' suitings ready-to-wear . . . an electric torch—touch the button and release sunlight?"

"No, dear old officer, captain and friend."

Sanders, looking over the top of his *Times*, hazarded a guess.

"Something to do with paint, Bones?"

Lieutenant Tibbetts's jaw dropped.

"How did you know that, Excellency?"

Sanders laughed softly.

"For three weeks before you went up-river you had been sounding me about decorating my fine house," he said dryly, "and for three weeks I had been trying to avert the disaster."

"Paint?" repeated Hamilton incredulously.

"Stencils," said Bones, and waded through the literature.

It took him till dinner-time to find the advertisement:

"MAKE YOUR HOME BEAUTIFUL

"Missouri Man makes $100.00 a week in spare time.   You can do the same."

It was an advertisement of "Eezy-Paynt":

"Not a Toy, but a
MONEY MAKER"

"As a matter of fact, Ham," confessed Bones, "I'd already ordered No. 3 outfit, hoping, dear old sir, that you wouldn't mind a little art."

"On the whole," said Sanders gravely, "I think it would be wiser to hand the outfit to Bosambo. I've no doubt he will make good use of it. And, on your way up-country, see T'chala and give him a tin of preserves. There, by the favour of heaven, is the only wise head in the Ochori!"

"Clever men are easy fallers," said Hamilton.

Sanders shook his head.

"T'chala is different. If he were a white man he would be remarkable. The man is a true philosopher."

"Tell me what a man is afraid of," said the cynical Hamilton, "and I will weigh up his philosophy!"

"He is afraid of nothing," said Sanders.

"The same as me," murmured Bones.

A month later, he explained to the fascinated paramount chief the art and practice of stencilling. They were on the forebridge of the *Zaire*, which had dropped Sanders at the Isisi city, and Bones had a whole day to spare.

"Lord, this is a wonder," breathed Bosambo. "For you put these little pieces of yellow paper and you jigger with your brush, and lo! there is a picture of a beautiful flower, so real that a man may smell it!"

"And a man on horseback," murmured Bones. "Don't forget the jolly old man on the jolly old horse, Bosambo. And a windmill, dear old savage."

Bosambo was too entranced by the new toy to be lured into English.

"Now all the people of the Ochori will see how great a magician I am," he said. "Even T'chala, the wise man, cannot paint a flower with his eyes shut."

This happened at a period when the Ochori, with every excuse in their favour, had denied the full quota of taxation to their master. There was a goat sickness and a blight on their corn; fish were scarce, and had moved to other waters. But the truth of it was that there was in the Ochori an epidemic of passive resistance, and the movement was so general that Bosambo hesitated to use force to extract from his tight-fisted nation the due which was his and Government's—especially his.

For the greater part of a week Bosambo sat with his wonderful box of stencils, and experimented and thought, and then one night his great *lokali* sent a message throughout the land, calling chiefs and headmen to a great palaver of state.

They came, albeit reluctantly, and prepared to contest the inevitable claims for further taxation, and they were surprised and delighted when Bosambo's head-men gave them private word that no question of taxes was to be discussed.

In the morning Bosambo sat in his chair of state under the thatched roof of the palaver house, and addressed the squatting half-moon of listeners.

"All people, listen!" he bellowed. "Sandi, who is my friend, and Tibbetti, who is like my brother, have made a palaver with me. And Sandi said this: 'There are good men in the Ochori and there are bad men. Put a mark upon the good, that when I meet them I may know and reward them. For this is the order of the great king who is my father.'"

The Ochori were suspicious and puzzled, and yet they understood the theory of markings; for did not all the petty chiefs wear silver medals about their necks in proof of their greatness? One old man, a notorious sinner, who had escaped the rope on two occasions by the fraction of an inch, rose up from the assembly and saluted.

"Bosambo," he said, "that is a good talk. Though people have spoken against me evilly, yet I love Sandi, as you well know. Mark me, that I may go back to my city and show my people this wonder."

"That indeed I will, Osaku," said Bosambo readily, "and the four hundred matakos that you shall pay me for this honour, and which I will send to our lord Sandi, will be as nothing to a man of your great wealth."

Osaku jibbed at this, but the possibilities were alluring. He compromised for three hundred matakos, and, lying flat on his stomach, allowed Bosambo to stencil a beautiful green windmill on his left shoulder-blade.

All day long Bosambo harangued and painted. Some of the headmen had brought no brass rods with them, and pleaded for credit; but the wily master of the Ochori was adamant to all such pleas. This question of decoration, he said in effect, was to be conducted on a strictly cash basis.

There were sceptics, but the majority, having seen the miracle performed, and having followed those who were marked and blessed, the better to observe the roses, windmills and baggy-trousered Dutchmen which ornamented their fellows, departed instantly for home to gather their treasures.

Many came who were not decorated. T'chala, the wise man of the Ochori, walked ten miles through the forest to witness the markings, but when Bosambo saw him he shook his head.

"These marks are for silly people who have no virtue, lord Bosambo," he said. "Now I am wise and I have knowledge of life and death, and I know that life is a dream and death is real. I neither seek reward nor punishment."

"I will do this for you because I love you," said Bosambo, who needed the testimonial of the wise man's approval, so that when the day came that Sanders called him to account he might point to T'chala as a disciple.

"Also, these magic signs will give you long life and great safety."

But T'chala smiled gravely and went away.

On the third day came the petty chief who was husband of M'lema, and he brought his wife with him. In return for a hundred matakos and a small bag of salt he had the privilege of bearing a glistening red cow across his stomach. But when he pushed forward his shrinking wife, Bosambo wiped the sweat from his forehead and put down his overworked paint-brush.

"This woman I will not mark," he said, knowing well the chief's foolish love for the girl; "for our lord Sandi has spoken against her."

"Bosambo," urged the chief, "she is a woman and, being a woman, has no sense. Now I will give you a thousand matakos and two goats if you put upon her the highest mark, so that when Sandi sees her he shall speak to her kindly."

Bosambo haggled for another goat, got it, and decorated her in a novel manner.

"Bosambo," protested the chief, "how can men see this wonderful mark? For she is not a shameless N'gombi woman who walks without proper clothing."

Bosambo recognised the force of the argument, and repeated his design on the nape of the woman's neck.

Later came O'fara, the penniless and friendless; and Bosambo, who had no sentiment, and was moreover running short of paint, waved her loftily to oblivion.

"These high mysteries are not for you, O'fara. Go find your woodman and let him bring me a bag of salt or such other treasures as woodmen bury in the ground."

So the sorrowful O'fara went back to the village and her solitude. And there she found T'chala the wise brooding on truth, and she sat down at his feet and told him of her poverty. T'chala was unusually distrait.

"I saw one mark like a great tree that Bosambo put upon an old man's chest, and this gave him long life," he mused, and glanced at the girl. "What need have you, woman, that Bosambo can fill? You are young—there you have all. Now I am a very old man, and I never pass a grave by the river's side but I stop to think what place will they dig for me. And life comes and goes like the sun. It is no sooner morning than it is night . . . a great red tree with branches that ran so."

She continued to lament her failure to be branded to the favour of Sandi.

"That I do not desire," he said, a trifle impatiently for such a holy man; "for Sandi loves me because of my wisdom, and I am very high above common men. . . . Life is a dream, but some men love dreaming. And death is real— but who desires reality when there are dreams? . . ."

News of the marking came to the little strip of land where the mad folks dwelt, and Bologa, the Akasava, chafing at his injustice, saw here a fulfilment of the God-man's promise. And a great idea taking shape in his mind, he carried out a plan. In the dead of the night he crept past the sleeping guard and, making his way to a fishing village, he stole a canoe and passed down the river till he came to his own land, to find that from one end of the country to the other the Akasava were in a state of ferment. He did not see the *Zaire* chasing north at full speed, her black smoke-stack belching sparks. Her decks were alive with soldiers, and about her two guns the shrapnel shells were stacked in rows, for the smell of war had reached the keen nostrils of Mr. Commissioner Sanders.

The story of the markings had gone up and down the river like wildfire, and each tribe had placed its own interpretation upon the favours shown to the Ochori. Bologa sought the king of the Akasava and expounded his theory.

"The God-man said this, that some should be marked as sheep and some as goats, and who are the sheep but the Ochori? For they were great cowards, as you well know, until Bosambo came. And this is the mystery, that all who are so marked shal be masters of our people and we shall be slaves to them, just as the God-man foretold."

"This is a bad palaver," said the king of the Akasava,

his face darkening. "Let us go up to these sheep and make a killing."

Sanders was only twenty miles away when the Akasava king gathered a thousand spears from his own city, and in the dark of a rainy night passed up the river to the first great village of the Ochori. The *lokali* rang out the alarm at daybreak, and Bosambo moved swiftly to the rescue of his ravaged domains. He flung his finest regiment through the smoking village and drove the Akasava spears in flight to their canoes and to the *Zaire* that came in sight as they paddled to mid-stream. In the heat of the afternoon Sanders accompanied a sobered Bosambo through the ruin. One house stood intact, and before this sat the unmarked O'fara.

"Lord, they did not kill me because I had no magic mark upon me. But M'lema they slew, also the chief, her husband, for they came upon us in grey-light and the people were sleeping."

"Where is T'chala, for this is his hut?" said Sanders. "And well I know that this wise man escaped the ruin."

Without a word she turned and walked into the hut, and Sanders followed.

T'chala was dead; the brass hilt of the broad-bladed elephant knife that killed him stuck out from the branches of a big red tree that was crudely painted on his breast.

"This magic painting I did because he asked me, and brought me camwood and oil, and showed me how the magic tree was made," said O'fara, "for he feared death very greatly."

X

THE SWEET SINGER

When Lieutenant Tibbetts had a great educational idea he usually reduced it to writing. The Residency saw little of him and heard nothing, for at meal-times he was very silent and taciturn, not to say irritable. He was like this when he elaborated his scheme for translating into the Bomongo tongue the nursery rhymes of his youth. For Bones was a restless educationalist, and if he was not acquiring knowledge he was never so happy as when he was passing along the fruits of his study.

His nursery rhymes were not too successful:

> "Miri-miri had a small goat
> With white hair
> When Miri-miri walked by the river
> The goat also walked.
> It went to all place behind Miri-miri"—

was the literal translation of "Mary had a little lamb," and Bones made an heroic effort to teach the children of the Isisi, the Akasava and the Ochori this legend.

"Lord," complained one of the petty chiefs of the Isisi, "Tibbetti came here and he called the children to a palaver, thus putting us men to shame. Then he made them say certain things about a white goat, and as you know, Sandi, a white goat is a terrible thing that brings bad luck. Therefore we kill them when they are born. And since our children have learned this magic saying, our crops have failed and the rubber trees have dried up. Also one of the little children has died of a cough and another has fallen into the river."

Nor was Bones more successful in his efforts to lead the immature minds of little Akasava boys to an appreciation of "Tom, Tom, the Piper's Son."

There was a complaint that he was teaching the Akasava children to steal pigs.

"I think you had better leave their education in the hands of the missionaries, Bones," said Sanders. "The trouble with our people is that they take things too literally."

So the Bomongo translations were scrapped, and he sought around for new inspiration.

"The man is tireless," said Hamilton. "Gosh! if I had his energy I'd work an engine! He spent all this morning reading me jokes from *Snappy Stuff*, which, I understand, is published in America. And Bones is getting ideas out of these wretched American journals—he called me a 'tight-wad' yesterday morning—I'll stand that, but if he calls me 'kid' again I'll search for the humane killer!"

Those paragraphs in the popular periodical press which are too short to tell the truth, exercise an uncanny fascination over a certain type of reader. Bones invariably reserved the page headed "Things that are not generally known" until the last. It was the old port and cigar of life's dinner. Hunched up at the table where his patent Ski-Lite reading lamp sometimes burnt and sometimes smoked, he read:

The amount of the National Debt in pennies would, if placed end to end, reach three times round the world.

———

There are more acres in Yorkshire than words in the Bible.

———

£500,000 per annum is earned in royalties by English playwrights.

———

Ink was invented by——etc., etc.

It may have been imagination on his part, or it may have been that the editor of "Things that are not generally known" had a working arrangement with the editor of "Queer Facts that are seldom realised," or that both were hand in glove with the gentleman who directed the page in another paper that was titled "Information in a Nutshell," but certainly Bones was always meeting that inspiring paragraph about authors' fees.

On a Sunday afternoon, when Sanders and the two soldiers were loafing on the stoep, waiting and praying for the inevitable thunderstorm which had threatened all day, Bones struggled up in his chair.

"Ham, old limpus, I'm goin' to write a play!"

Bones usually chose such moments as these for his most startling announcements. The heat and the airlessness of the muggiest day never reduced his mind to cabbage-level or sapped his vital juices.

Hamilton turned a moist face and a pleading eye in his direction.

"Wait till it's cooler, Bones," he begged. "Be a good fellow and shut up till the rain comes—I thought I heard thunder just now."

"Off?" suggested Bones. "Thunder off, dear old dramatist?"

Hamilton groaned.

"Why not a play about the Territories?" demanded Bones. "This is the plot. A young an' good-lookin' but perfectly jolly old lieutenant—the hero, Ham—is fearfully hated by his naughty old captain, Ham. When things go wrong it's always the jolly old lieutenant who gets people out of a mess and always the wicked old skipper who gets the credit. Do you follow me, Ham?"

Hamilton closed his eyes and moaned.

"Then a nice old lady comes to the station, Ham—beautiful eyes, beautiful hair, beautiful figure, an' naturally she falls desperately in love with the jolly old subaltern. Listenin', Ham?"

Hamilton's eyes were closed.

"Listenin', dear old sir?"

Hamilton moaned again.

"But this jolly old subaltern is fearfully honourable. He knows that—oh, I forgot to tell you, Ham—that this beautiful old lady's father doesn't like the jolly old officer an' that she's really not his daughter. What I mean is, there's a villain named Captain Dark. Now, how do you think, Ham, old sir, this jolly young subaltern saves the girl?"

"Which girl?" asked Hamilton drowsily.

"The girl I'm talking about. A ghost warns her!"

"And what does she do to the goat?" murmured his superior.

Bones made a noise indicative of annoyance.

"Ghost—G—O—S—T, ghost. He's physic—the jolly old subaltern, I mean."

Hamilton opened one eye.

"Has physic?"

"Tut, tut, Ham! Physic! He could see ghosts an' things like that—call 'em up, dear old officer." Bones snapped his finger in illustration. "Ghost, ghost, ghost! an' up they popped. This play will make a fortune, Ham. There hasn't been a physic hero before——"

"Psychic, you poor frog!" snarled Hamilton. "And let me sleep, will you?"

A flicker of white lightning behind the Residency wood, a rumble that rolled loudly to a deafening, head-splitting crash, and Hamilton opened his eyes.

"There she blows!" he said cheerfully. "Oh, smell the lov-erly wind!"

The dust on the parade-ground was swirling in little spirals, the roar of the distant rain came to them before the first big drops fell.

Sanders woke from a doze, reached for his cigar-case and lit a black cheroot, a smile in his tired eyes.

"This naughty old father, Ham, wants the girl to marry the other fellow, an' of course the handsome old lieutenant knows this an' he jolly well won't have anything to do with her——"

"Come inside, you talkative devil," said Hamilton, rising lazily as the rain came down. "And if you put me in a play I'll break your infernal head!"

With Bones, to think was to act. Before the storm had passed he was committing to paper his immense idea.

Scene I. A well-known Residency.

Enter Lieutenant Harold Darcey.

Lieut. H. D. Ah. Nobody here. Nobodey here. The golly old place is deserted. Now for a wisky and soder. (*Pours out a wisky and soder*). Ah! I mustnt waist time. My studys my studdis studdies must come first.

(*Enter Dorman Mackalyster, a yung and lutiful girl lovely eyes &c.*)

D. M.—Oh, I didn't know you were here were here Lt. Darcey. Oh how I love you.

Lt. H. D.—It can never be dear old Dorman our ways ways lay far apart you are pleged to annother anotther Fairwell. I am Physic. I know that it can never be.

D. M.—Oh do not leaf me Harold. Their is something you ort aught ourt to know. My farther is not my father is not my farther but a foundling that adopted me when I was but a child.

(*Enter Captain Dark.*)

Capt. D.—Ah what are you doing alown with this man alone. Curse you Harold I will rune ruing ruin your life.

Somewhere about midnight, when Hamilton was going to bed, Bones brought the first act.

"Read it, Ham, old sir," he said a little nervously. "Just tell me what you think of it. Give me your candid view, Ham. Personally, I think it's the best play I ever wrote."

"How many have you written?" asked his astonished superior.

"It's the first, dear old critic," replied Bones shamelessly.

Hamilton turned the ink-stained manuscript.

"I'll read it in bed," said the mendacious man.

In the morning he had time to read the first act.

"It's a rotten play," was his criticism at breakfast. "The spelling is quite normal in places, but otherwise it has no redeeming features."

Bones sneered.

"Ah ha! You recognised yourself, dear old Captain Dark! Naturally, dear old sorebones, you didn't like it. But when you see the second act——"

"There will be no second act," said Hamilton firmly.

"You don't know old Bones," said Bones, who did know old Bones.

The veto came from an unexpected quarter. Sanders objected mildly and gently to the development of the plot.

"If you write about a party of American scientists being refused admission to the Territory and it gets into print, I shall be kicked," he said. "It is highly dramatic, but it is bad history."

Bones started to rewrite the second act—and a young dramatist who starts in to rewrite second acts usually writes no more. As for the affair with the American expedition——

All British officials are inclined to be a little supercilious to the foreigner and disobliging to their own kind.

Mr. Commissioner Sanders was not popular with outsiders, because he hated interference of all kinds and turned a hard face to all strangers. Across the Territories might have been written in letters a mile high. "No admittance except on business." He had turned down more exploration parties, more prospectors and more traders than any ten commissioners in Africa. He had had sermons preached against him in missionary circles, and had been most offensively prayed for; he had been reported and paragraphed, and very unpleasant leading articles had been written about him. But his policy of non-interference was one that had the sneaking approval of his superiors, though occasionally he had found himself in conflict with the powers.

Notably in the case of the Cress-Rainer expedition, which set out from the United States with the official benison of the British Ambassador. They were specimen-hunting, and undoubtedly the Territory was rich in strange mammals and unclassified bugs. .But Sanders had shut the door, and rightly. It was the time of the big war which decimated the nations and crept southward, even to the doors of the Residency. There was a rumpus about this, but in the weary end Sanders had triumphed and the expedition went down to Angola.

Yet Sanders liked Americans, and, for all his so-called

antagonism to "the work," loved one missionary who was not only American but of German origin. He would have given half his pay to have kept this homely, middle-aged woman under his eyes. But this was not to be.

When Mrs. Kleine of Cincinnati left the Isisi people there were loud lamentations, for she was a God-mama so well beloved that a whole nation accompanied her in their canoes for the first thirty miles of her journey. She was a practical, hard-headed Christian, with all the fine qualities of her ancestors. And she left the Isisi because the work was too easy, and she went up into the horrible Ojubi country, electing to live and die in a place where white men seldom came. And there she procured an even greater devotion from her flock than she had known in the Isisi. She was a great singer of hymns, had a beautiful contralto voice, and was famous through the three great tribes; and when her health broke down and she decided to return to the United States, the people of Ojubi took counsel together, and one morning, when she was asleep, her favourite lay preacher, with tears streaming down his face, went into her hut and speared her—so swiftly and so skilfully that "only her eyelids fluttered a little."

Sanders was eighty miles away when he picked up the news from the *lokali*, and he made a forced march through forest and swamp and came up to the Ojubi village in the first flush of dawn, when the beautiful little flowers that Mama had planted before her hut were a blaze of glory.

He sat down, a tired, soiled-looking man, and held his palaver.

"Lord," said the slayer, "the Mama was very beautiful to us, and so we killed her, that her holy body might stay with us always."

This was not only the slayer's view, but the view of all the people, even of the chief who dominated the village and the district around.

Sanders was not shocked; he was not angry; he was a little sad at the thought of this good life that had been cut short. He hanged the murderer out of hand, and the man went to his doom singing a doleful hymn, and approved by his fellow-citizens.

The chief he sent to the village of irons and appointed his successor. There were other palavers to be held; poor Mrs. Kleine's effects to be packed and dispatched to her home town; and on the last day of his stay Sanders called the new chief aside and gave him a few words of counsel.

"This is a terrible thing which your people have done, chief," he said. "More terrible because they think there is no sin in it. And although all the world knows that the Ojubi are a silly people, yet they are more foolish than men suppose."

"Lord, there was no folly in sending Mama to the spirits," said the new chief astonishingly. "And well we know this, because last night many of our young men heard her singing her beautiful songs in the forest. For she told us that people did not die, and if people do not die how can they be killed?"

The Commissioner had neither the time nor the desire to argue abstract questions of theology. The story of the singing voice he dismissed as an inevitable invention, and he went down to the Isisi to break the news to the people, and, incidentally, to nip in the bud any plan of reprisal. And it was well he did so, for the tidings had already reached the Isisi, and a small but select expedition was in course of forming to settle with the Ojubi people, though three hundred miles of river and forest separated the two tribes.

There were certain unpleasant plans to deal with the chief of the Ojubi, and one of these was to take him out on the Island of Snakes, where the mad woman lived.

Where the great river meets the rushing waters of the Kasava is a little pear-shaped island that is called the Place of Snakes. With good reason, for certain big snakes live comfortably here, there being many trees where vampire bats sleep in clusters by day—and bats are good eating for the long, glistening things that climb trees so slowly that they do not seem to move.

The island had had one inhabitant for many years. Here lived a woman who loved snakes and bats and the strange other things that only she understood. Lobili was her name, and she was a foreigner, having come to the country in the year that Sanders was on his leave.

She was rich, not in stock and salt or rods, as people in this land are rich, but by all accounts in money. There was no reason why Sanders should visit her, and many reasons why he should not. The island stood in a place where strong currents and cross-eddies made an anchorage difficult. He knew she was there, guessed her to be a coast woman who had come back to the land of her ancestors for some reason, and was content to have his reports of her from neighbouring chiefs and from his spies, who knew most things.

Amongst others, he learned that she smoked, and that her house was a handsome hut erected by Isisi workmen whom she had bribed to venture into this dreadful place; and that she paid her taxes to the chief; and that, when she raised her hand, certain snakes fell dead. He gave the usual discount to this miracle, attributed to all who are credited as graduates in witchcraft.

The day he saw her was the day he met her. From the deck of the *Zaire*, as it swung round in the current, he saw a grey-haired figure standing by the edge of the water, holding the end of a fishing line. There was a pipe in her mouth and she raised her hand in salute as he passed.

He was on his way to the Isisi village, which is sited opposite the island, to inquire into an irregularity, for Obisi, son of a petty chief, had been taken out of the water half dead, with a big lump on his forehead. The man was a notorious ne'er-do-well, who hunted when the game came so close that he could send his arrows flying from the bed on which he loved to lie, and fished when he could squat in a canoe and direct his first wife in her spearing. He showed energy only in one pursuit: he was a conscienceless thief and had dwelt for a year in the village of irons. Obisi was in bad case now, for there was a great swelling on his forehead and a tiny punctured wound.

"Lord, I went to the island where the mad woman lives," he wailed, "and she came to me and spoke evil words, and when I answered her she put out her hand and I felt a terrible pain in my head."

"At what hour did you go to the island?" asked Sanders, and the man hesitated.

"Lord, it was in the darkness of the night," he said, "for I was ashamed that any of my friends should see me on my way to speak to this mad woman."

Sanders had to deal with primitive people, and he was invariably blunt and to the point.

"You went there to steal!" he accused, and Obisi denied the charge mechanically.

Sanders examined the wound and was puzzled. He naturally discounted stories of magic, but here was certainly a mysterious happening that called for further inquiry. With some difficulty he landed on the island, and, walking warily along the well-trod path, his automatic in his hand (for he hated snakes), he came at last to the big hut where the old woman sat—a big, broad-shouldered woman who was neither Isisi nor Akasava.

She waited patiently, her hands folded in her lap.

"Lobili, I see you," he said. "Now they tell me a strange word about you. . . ."

He repeated Obisi's story and she listened without a word. When he had finished:

"Lord, this man is worse than a thief," she said. "He came to this island last night, and I think that one of the snakes that hang on the trees struck him."

Which was a plausible explanation.

"Why do you live here all alone, Lobili? You are a woman and there are dreadful things on this island."

"They are not dreadful to me, lord," she said, and made a little whistling noise. And then, to Sanders's horror, he saw a flat, spade-shaped head come obliquely round the corner of the door, heard the angry hiss and whipped round, his pistol extended.

"Lord, he will not hurt you, for I have taken the poison from him," she said, with the ghost of laughter in her brown eyes.

She made a clicking noise with her lips and the snake vanished.

"I am afraid of none of these things," she said. "There are worse there"—she pointed to the Isisi bank. "For in a certain place in the forest are big snakes that will crush a man to death and kill him with a blow of their great heads. And there dwell also men who do evil for the love of evil."

Sanders looked at her sharply, for the rumour had reached him also. He did not question her, for she hinted of something about which no native will speak.

He returned to the *Zaire* and to the village, and made a few inquiries about certain strangers in the depth of the forest.

The Isisi people watched the *Zaire* apprehensively for the next few days. It went aimlessly up and down the river, called at small fishing villages, made visits to unfrequented middle islands and to isolated settlements. And everywhere he heard the same story. Men had disappeared mysteriously; fishermen had gone out in their boats and had not returned; in one case a woman had gone into the forest and had vanished.

He was conscious that not only were the seen villages watching, but unseen eyes in the forest followed the *Zaire* from place to place.

When at last his ship paddled out of sight down-stream there were many relieved hearts in the Isisi.

Sanders brought the *Zaire* to the little quay and gave orders that steam was to be kept and the boat held ready to leave at a minute's notice, and when he met Hamilton he spoke neither of the wounded Obisi nor yet of the snake-woman.

"There is a chopping palaver up in the Isisi," he said, in

a tone of despair. "And I only hanged D'firo-fusu six months ago!"

Hamilton whistled. "The swine!" he said softly.

The Isisi, the N'gombi and part of the Akasava are cannibal people. They were always very frank about it. Man was meat, and there was the end of it. Also, warriors fought better for the meal that followed victory. Slowly but surely, the new law had ground out the practice. Many men had been hanged on high trees; many were sent in irons to work for Government; whip and rope had changed the habits of the people—but now and again appeared a wandering band of devotees to the old custom, and behind them was a strong business end.

"Bones must go up in the *Zaire* ostensibly on a marriage palaver—there is one waiting settlement at the Ochori city. He must take as few men as possible so as not to frighten the birds. We'll follow on the *Wiggle* with all the men we can spare—you'll want machine-guns, Hamilton, by the way. I think I have located them."

So Bones went up, and he took his unfinished play with him, and in quiet woodings the adventures of the "physic" Harold and the evil Captain Dark were developed so eerily that there were times when he leapt up at the sound of a breaking twig.

Navigation was an art which Lieutenant Tibbetts had never thoroughly acquired. The river was treacherous, never quite what it seemed on its surface, and sandbanks had a habit of coming and going, so that where was a deep channel overnight was a boat-trap in the morning.

Going up was a fairly simple business, for the river ran five knots after the rain, and the *Zaire* made ten knots, which meant that when it was doing five knots against the black water he was speeding.

But this trip of Bones had one exasperating feature which was unusual. Every twenty miles along the river was a wooding, where great stacks of chores and felled timber awaited the pleasure of Sandi. The men who cut these offered their service and were exempt from other taxation. Roughly speaking, a week's work once a year was the extent of their labours, for the woodings were chosen in rotation, and sometimes the chores were not brought on board the *Zaire* until a year after the billets had been cut.

And in the first wooding whereat Bones stopped, intending to spend the night—there was no wood. The nearest stock was twenty miles away. Night was coming on, and hereabouts navigation is not to be lightly undertaken in the dark. Bones sent a Houssa through the darkening forest and summoned before him the chief of the little village whose task it was to supply the labour.

This man was very glib. "Lord," he said, "Sandi himself took our wood two moons and one ago, and because my young men have been sick and very weak we have not cut down the trees——'

Bones cut his explanation short. On the *Zaire* was a little book in which was kept a very accurate record of the woodings visited, and this was known as "57," and the *Zaire* had not tied up to the steep banks of the forest for nearly eighteen months.

"You're a naughty old story-teller," said Bones, annoyed, and then, in Bomongo: "You shall cut and pile twice the wood I require before my return, Kibili. Also, I will draw taxation from you—so many strings of fish and so much salt. Have this when I return."

The chief was a little terrified, crossed his arms over his thin chest and clasped his sides, a gesture of supreme unhappiness.

"Lord, the fish you may have and the salt also, but the wood I cannot give you, because my young men are sick, and, lord, we are terribly frightened because of the great spirits which dwell hereabouts, as your lordship knows."

"O fool!" said the aggravated young man. "What spirits are there in the world?"

At that moment there flashed into his mind the memory of his "physic" hero, and a ghost half-raised (on paper) in his cabin.

"There are many spirits here, Tibbetti," said the chief in a hushed voice, "and because of them my young men are afraid to come into this part of the wood. For here is heard the voice of the singing mama."

"Singing——"

Bones had known the singing mama, and a cold chill crept down his spine. The little chief saw his advantage and followed it up.

"Often we have heard her beautiful songs as she walks through the dark woods," he said; "and sometimes we fear for her because of the Killers——"

He had betrayed himself: the young officer saw him squirm in an ecstasy of fear.

Now, Bones in his leisure and private moments was quite different from the Bones on duty. His blue eyes narrowed until they seemed closed. He had reached the jumping-off place where he left behind all that was not deadly earnest.

"Speak, man," he said softly, "and tell me of these Killers who live in the forest and chop men."

Now he knew why there was no wood to carry him to the next post: fear of the Killers, who pick off solitary workmen and prey on the little bands of woodmen.

"O, ko! I have talked too much!" gasped the chief, his face a mottled grey. "Let me talk with my people, lord."

Bones nodded. He went back to the boat and flew a pigeon to Sanders, then called Ali Mahmet, the corporal of his six soldiers.

"Two men will stay on the puc-a-puc and stand by the hawsers. Yoka the engineer and his man shall keep steam ready. You and your four men will come ashore with fifty rounds and go where I go."

Then he went on the land and the chief was waiting to speak with him.

"This is the truth, Tibbetti," he said. "The Killers live in the forest half a night's journey away. There are two hands of them"—he held up two hands with the fingers extended. "Now I think with your fine soldiers you may catch them, for it is true that we are afraid. And once before, when the Killers came here, in the days of my father, they took my own brother away with them . . ."

Bones listened to the tragic history with great patience.

"You shall walk before me, chief," he said, "and if you are a Killer man and lead me and my fine soldiers into danger, you shall walk in hell this night."

There was a very definite path through the forest, it appeared, and Bones remembered that once he had followed the first part of it in quest of a certain white weakling who had broken the laws. He spent the rest of the day coaching his men, anxiously awaiting news from Sanders. If he lost this opportunity he might miss his quarry altogether.

He waited until the night came, a cool night of stars, and fell in his little party. Kibili, the chief, led the way, and behind him came Bones. They marched in silence for an hour, and then the man called a halt. From time to time as they walked, Bones slipped his compass from his pocket and examined the illuminated dial. It is next to impossible to get an exact compass bearing on the march, but he saw enough to realise that they had diverged from the northern track and were walking in a half-circle eastwards. So far from entering the forest, they were keeping an almost parallel course with the river. When they halted he confirmed this. They were now moving towards the Isisi city. He put the compass back in his pocket, and, taking out his automatic, kept his thumb on the safety catch.

For a minute he considered the advisability of returning to the *Zaire*. But if the agreed plan was in operation, Sanders, who was only ten hours behind him, would be near the wooding by now. If he were tied up at a lower depot he would certainly send a runner through the forest in search of news.

The wood was very silent and still, and Bones, in a brief moment, thought of ghosts and shivered.

"March," he said in a low tone, and the little column went on.

Again they stopped at the end of an hour. They were moving inland, but still they were within easy reach of the river. The *Zaire* could have kept pace with them if he had only understood the direction of the chase. For the moment his suspicion of the guide was mechanical rather than acute. The man might be following the safer path to the lair of the Red Men.

Another two hours brought them to rising ground.

"Lord, on the other side of this is the Place of the Red Men," whispered the guide. He was reeking with perspiration, which was partly due to fear.

Bones called Ali Mahmet to him.

"Let the men fix their little swords," he said in a low voice. "There must be no shooting till I speak."

The bayonets had been blacked in the smoke of an oil wick before they left the boat. He heard the click-click as they slipped into their sockets . . . when he turned again to the guide he had vanished. As silent as the forest about them, he had gone from view.

Bones thumbed down the safety catch of his pistol and grinned mirthlessly into the night.

"Shoulder to shoulder in a circle, Ahmet Ali!" he said, and felt his way to the nearest man.

At that instant he heard a guttural Arabic oath and the "flug" of a bayonet striking home, and simultaneously somebody caught him by the ankles and he went down to earth with a crash that knocked the breath out of him. Twice he fired at the body that fell upon him, and felt the convulsive wriggle that followed, and then something struck him on the side of the head and he went silly.

He was standing when he came to his senses, and he could feel the warm wet blood that was rolling leisurely from his cheek. Somebody held him; his gun was gone, and he heard a man sobbing with pain near his feet.

"Let us take them to the Killing Place," said a voice,

and then another called Kibili by name, only they used the
N'gombi equivalent, which is "N'gosobo."

"He is dead," said a third voice. "Tibbetti chopped
him with the little gun that says 'ha ha!'"

The first speaker grunted something and the party
moved on. Bones listened to the footfalls and presently
distinguished them all. His men were still alive; he heaved
a sigh of thankfulness and, appreciating the small cause
there was for relief, grinned again. His hands were tied
native fashion, which meant that they were fastened so
tightly that presently his hands would begin to swell. If he
could persuade them to let his hands go free there was a
small Browning in the inside pocket of his shirt.

"O man!" he called. "Why do you tie me, for you
have my little gun that says 'ha ha!' and you are many."

"A tied man does not cut his hands," was the ominous
answer—the old cannibal slogan.

He tried to reach his shirt-pocket, but the rough native
rope that held him was passed under his legs and knotted
to his elbows behind.

Crossing a ridge, Bones had a momentary glimpse of
the river, and far away the twinkling light of a fire.

"Tibbetti, this night you die," said a voice. "There
was a little dog who followed a leopard into the wood,
and all the time the leopard followed him."

Silence followed, and then unexpectedly the unknown
leader called a halt.

"I hear," he said, and they stood listening . . . a sharp
steel point touched Bones's throat.

"It is nothing——"

Almost as he spoke, the voice came from the wood—
the voice of a woman singing.

> "While shepherds watched their flocks by night,
>   All seated on the ground,
>   The angel of the Lord came down,
>   And glory shone around,"

Clear as a bell, yet soft and unspeakably sweet the voice
sounded. It was near them.

Bones went cold: he had never heard the voice of Mama Kleine, but this was an American. . . .

"O, ko! what is that?" asked a hoarse voice.

"It is the spirit of Mama-Jesu," came an answer.

They waited, but there was no other sound but the thud of hearts beating fiercely.

"We are there," said somebody. "Let us light the fire."

Bones heard the sound of wet leaves being brushed aside, and a dull glowing circle appeared on the earth. An armful of dry brushwood was thrown on the hidden fire, smoked fragrantly for a moment, and then burst into flames.

And now Bones saw—not ten, but forty of the Red Men, mainly N'gombi. One who seemed to be in some position of authority had a great bump on his forehead, and him the others addressed as Obisi.

Bones looked round for the survivors of his party and found them more or less intact, and wondered why they had been spared. It was Obisi who supplied the answer, as though he had interpreted the questioning glance.

"The live goat walks," he said, "but the dead goat we must carry."

"Sellin' us on the hoof," said Bones in English, and was hysterically pleased with his ghastly jest.

"You, Tibbetti, we will kill because you are white and nobody would buy you," said Obisi.

He took from the hands of one of the men a sickle-shaped weapon, broad in the blade and crudely engraved.

"This——" he said, and then he fell down.

Bones heard the ping! and the smack of the thing that struck him, but he was unprepared for the collapse of his executioner. A man yelled in fright and ran to the prostrate Obisi and turned him on his back.

"This is magic!" he yelled, and his hand was fumbling for the sickle knife when:

Ping!

The man dropped on his knees, his hand at his side, grimacing horribly.

From somewhere along the forest path came the sound of shots, and presently three naked forms flew into the light of the fire and screamed something over their shoulders. Bones heard the words and almost swooned.

"Speak well for me, Tibbetti," gasped a man, and nacked in two the rope that bound him—and he was a lucky man. The bullet that whistled past just missed him as he ducked his head to cut the last strands.

"All right, sir!" yelled Bones, as Sanders's pistol was raised.

"Thank the good Lord——" began Sanders.

Then came the eerie interruption. From the shadows of the wood came the voice of the sweet singer:

"Now thank we all our God . . ."

Sanders stared into the shadows.

"For the love of heaven!" he gasped, and then came the most astonishing incident of that night.

Into view, walking very slowly, came the grey-haired snake-woman.

"O Lobili——" began Sanders, and she laughed, a low, chuckling laugh of delight

"I'm afraid I'm not called Lobili," she said, and Sanders could have dropped, for this handsome old negress spoke English. "I'm Dr. Selina Grant, of Gregorytown University, Curator and Lecturer on Biology. We simply had to get somebody in this country, Mr. Sanders. My colour helped a lot, I guess, but it required a great deal of heartsearching before a woman of my age consented to assume the scanty attire of the indigenous native."

"Good God!" said Sanders hollowly, and pinched himself to make sure that he was awake. "You're—you're a negress?"

She nodded laughingly.

"Sure; that's how the Lord made me. My father was a doctor in Charlestown and my mother was pure Bantu. Bomongo I learnt in six months from a missionary who was on leave back home. I guess it came natural. It was kind of lonely—I've been here three years—and if I hadn't wandered around singing, I'd have forgotten what the American language sounded like! And, Mr. Sanders, I've got the dandiest lot of unclassified Ophidia you could wish to see—you must come to my island and inspect my viporum. . . ."

Sanders took off his helmet and held out his hand.

"Shake, doctor," he said; and Dr. Selina Grant stuck the air-pistol into her belt and gripped his hand in her big palm.

"Excuse me, dear old ma'am." Bones found his voice. "It was you singin'?"

"Sure!" said Selina.

"An' your jolly old air-gun——?"

"Air-pistol—it's the only weapon I've had, but it's mighty useful."

"Excuse me, ma'am," said Bones, agitated.

"I'll bet none of you boys has got the makings?" she asked. "This pipe-smoking's too primitive for Selina."

Bones found her a cigarette and lit it for her.

"You're the first native lady I've done that for," he said. It was indeed the most novel experience of his life.

Made and printed in France.
7565-6-48. — Imp. CRÉTÉ, Corbeil. — C. O. L. 31-1631.

A LIST OF PAN BOOKS